No
Fixed
Address

Also by Susin Nielsen

My Messed-up Life

Optimists Die First

The Reluctant Journal of Henry K. Larsen

We Are All Made of Molecules

Word Nerd

NO FIXED ADDRESS

A NOVEL BY SUSIN NIELSEN

ANDERSEN PRESS

This edition published in 2020 by
Andersen Press Limited
20 Vauxhall Bridge Road
London SW1V 2SA
www.andersenpress.co.uk

2 4 6 8 10 9 7 5 3 1

First published in hardback in 2018 by Andersen Press

British Library Cataloguing in Publication Data available.

ISBN 978 1 78344 832 6

Typeset by Palimpsest Book Production Ltd, Falkirk, Stirlingshire

Printed and bound in Great Britain
by Clays Ltd, Elcograf S.p.A.

I dedicated my first novel to Eleanor Nielsen, and I dedicate this, my sixth, to her too. Both feature single-parent moms of only children – same as me and my mom. But the similarities stop there. Mom, whether or not you consistently felt it yourself, you always made the ground feel safe beneath my feet. And still do.

November 27, 12:05 a.m.

My leg jiggled up and down. I shifted from one bum cheek to the other. My palms felt damp and my heart was pounding. 'I've never been interrogated before.'

'You're not being interrogated, Felix. We're just having a chat.'

'Are you going to record it?'

'Why would I do that?'

'It's how they do it on TV.'

'We're not on TV.'

The cold from the metal chair seeped through my pyjama bottoms. 'Do cops watch cop shows?'

'Of course.'

'But isn't that like bringing your work home with you?'

Constable Lee smiled. Her teeth were very straight. My Powers of Observation, or P.O.O., told me that she came from a middle-class family, one that could afford an orthodontist. My P.O.O. also told me she enjoyed her food: the buttons on her uniform were strained to the max. 'Not really,' she answered. 'It's escapism for us, too.

And we get to shout at the TV if they do something totally bogus.'

'Like what?'

'Like record this type of conversation. We only record a conversation if someone has been charged with a crime, or is a suspect in a crime.'

'Are you recording Astrid right now?'

'I can't answer that.'

Oh boy. I hardly ever cry, but all of a sudden I thought I might burst into tears, right in front of a cop. I think she could tell, because she added, 'I highly doubt it.'

I breathed in. I breathed out. I sat up straight. I tried to look calm and dignified even though I knew my blond curls were sticking out in all directions, because until everything went so terribly wrong I'd been in bed. Plus I was wearing my ancient Minions pyjamas, which were juvenile and way too small. Constable Lee and her partner hadn't given us time to change. 'I'd like to call my lawyer,' I said.

'Let me guess – you got that from TV, too.'

'Yes.'

'Do you have a lawyer?'

'No. But legally I'm allowed one, right?'

'Except you don't need one. You haven't done anything wrong.'

'So I could just leave?'

'I suppose. But where would you go?'

I thought about Dylan. And Winnie. Then I remembered

that I'd told them I never wanted to see them again. 'When will they be done talking to Astrid?'

'Soon, I'm sure.' She stared at me, clicking her pen, open, shut, open, shut. 'Mind if I ask why you don't call her Mom?'

'She says it's too hierarchical.' I scanned the huge room, full of desks and a handful of people, for the hundredth time. For the hundredth time, I didn't spot Astrid.

It'll be OK, I thought-messaged her, because she's always telling me she'll receive anything I send her. I don't believe that any more, but under the circumstances, it was worth a shot. 'For the record,' I said to Constable Lee, 'Astrid is a great parent.'

'Good to know.' She tapped on her keyboard. 'I'm going to ask you a few questions, OK?'

'OK.'

'Let's start with your full name.'

'Felix Fredrik Knutsson.'

She typed it into her computer. 'Age?'

'Thirteen. Well, almost. Twelve and three-quarters.'

'Mom's full name?'

'Astrid Anna Knutsson.'

'Address?'

I looked down at my feet. I wore rubber boots, no socks; there hadn't been time to search for a pair.

Constable Lee leaned towards me. Her shoulders were rounded. She did not have good posture. 'When we answered your call tonight, Felix, it did appear as if you were both living there.'

Oh, how I longed for my mom. She would have a plausible-sounding explanation. But I'm not like her. I'm not a natural-born stretcher of the truth.

So I continued to stare at the floor.

Constable Lee started typing, even though I hadn't said a word.

'Felix,' she said gently, 'you can talk to me . . .'

'I'm hungry.'

'Of course. I should have asked.' She pushed herself up from her desk and hitched her trousers up around her belly. 'We're talking vending-machine snacks. Hope that's OK. Any allergies? Any preferences?'

'No allergies. No preferences. Although I am partial to anything cheese-flavoured.'

Constable Lee walked across the big room. I glanced around. A couple of cops were at their desks. One was reading *Popular Mechanics* and another was dozing.

I swivelled Constable Lee's computer screen towards me. It was an official-looking report.

Name: Felix Fredrik Knutsson
Age: 12
Parent/Guardian: Astrid Anna Knutsson
Address: NFA

I'm pretty good at figuring out acronyms, and this one, given the context, came to me almost right away.

No fixed address.

I felt a ripple of dread. Astrid had warned me over and over: 'No one can find out where we live.' Until tonight, I'd broken the rule only once.

Our cover was blown. I tried to tell myself it wasn't my fault. I'd had no choice; I had to call the cops. If I hadn't, who knows what would have happened?

Still. The bad guys got away. And who was at the police station? The innocent victims. Us.

Two bags of Cheezies landed on the desk in front of me, along with a can of Coke. 'Aren't we a nosy parker,' Constable Lee said as she swivelled the computer screen back.

'No one can agree on the origin of that expression,' I said. 'Some people think it came from an archbishop in the fifteen hundreds named Parker, who asked too many questions. Other people think that's hooey, since the phrase didn't appear till the end of the nineteenth century.' I knew I was rambling, but I couldn't help it.

'You are a fount of knowledge.'

'My mom says I store facts like a squirrel stores nuts.'

Constable Lee tore open a bag of crisps and popped one into her mouth. 'Now. You have to believe me when I say I'm here to help.'

I wanted to believe her. But I kept thinking of my mom, who snorted like a pig whenever a police car drove past. Who liked to say 'Never trust the Man'.

'Which man?' I'd asked when I was younger.

'*The* Man. It's an expression. It means any man or woman who's in a position of authority.'

So all I said to Constable Lee was, 'Thanks. But we don't need any help.'

'Really?'

'Really. We'll be moving very soon.'

'Yeah? Where?'

'I don't know yet. But I'm coming into some money. The only question is how much.'

'An inheritance?'

'No.'

'Selling some valuables?'

'No.'

'Robbing a bank?'

'Very funny. No.'

'So where's this money coming from?'

'A game show.'

'Well, now I'm intrigued. Tell me more.'

'About the show?'

Constable Lee put her feet up on her desk. 'About everything.'

I studied her face. My P.O.O. told me she was a decent person. Maybe if she knew the truth, she would see that we'd done nothing wrong.

So I poured a bunch of Cheezies down my throat.

Then I told Constable Lee the whole truth and nothing but.

A Brief History of Homes

We haven't always lived in a van.

That only started four months ago. B.V. – Before Van – we lived in a four-hundred-square-foot basement. Before that, we lived in a six-hundred-square-foot apartment. Before that, we actually owned an eight-hundred-square-foot apartment.

And before any of that, we lived with Mormor.

Mormor's House

Mormor means 'mother's mother' in Swedish. She was my grandma. Astrid and I lived with her in her bungalow in New Westminster, just outside Vancouver, until I was six going on seven. Her house was crammed full of knick-knacks from Sweden; she must have had fifty red and blue wooden Dalarna horses. She also had a large *tomte* collection.

Tomtar, plural for *tomte*, are mischievous gnomelike creatures in Swedish folklore. They watch over you and protect your family. But if you don't treat them with respect, they can also be cruel. They might play a trick on you, or steal your things, or even kill your farm animals.

Mormor gave me my own *tomte* on my fifth birthday, one she'd made herself out of felt. He was ten centimetres tall with a long white beard, a red cone-shaped hat and a red jacket. 'Your own protector,' she said. I named him Mel.

Mormor looked after me when Astrid was at work. My mom had two jobs back then: she taught an evening painting class in Vancouver at Emily Carr University, and she answered phones in an insurance office. 'Once I've saved enough,' she'd say to me, 'we'll get our own place.' She didn't like living with Mormor.

But I did. Mormor took me to the park in the mornings, and in the afternoons I played imaginary games like Pirate Ship and Fort and Outer Space while she watched her shows. Drew, Maury, Ellen, Phil, Judge Judy, the women on *The View* – they felt like friends. And I have Mormor to thank for introducing me to *Who, What, Where, When* with Horatio Blass. It was her favourite show, and it became mine, too.

Mormor was what's called a Lutheran, and she read me Bible stories (but it had to be our little secret because Astrid said organised religion was the cause of all the world's woes and she'd broken up with the church a long time ago). We made *pepparkakor,* which is Swedish for 'gingerbread', and Mormor let me eat balls of dough. At naptime she let me curl up on her cushiony lap and doze while she watched TV.

When I had just turned six, I woke up from one of those naps to find that Mormor was sleeping, too. This was not unusual; she often took a mid-afternoon snooze. So I got up and played quietly on the floor with my Brio train set, which had belonged to my mom and her brother when they were little. After an hour or so, when Mormor still hadn't woken up, I gave her a tiny poke. Her head slumped further down onto her chest. Her skin was grey and cool to the touch. I noticed a dark stain underneath her. It was wet.

I started to giggle, delighted. 'Mormor, you peed your pants!' Up to that moment I'd been the only one in our household to pee their pants.

She didn't answer.

'Mormor?' I knew something wasn't right. But I was little. I had not yet fully developed my P.O.O.

I called my mom. She called 911 and came straight home. But there was nothing anyone could do.

I missed Mormor a lot, and I know my mom did, too. For months afterwards I slept in Astrid's room, and I brought Mel in every night so he could watch over us while we slept. I wasn't taking any chances.

Our Brief Brush with Homeownership

Mormor left everything to my mom. It wasn't as much as Astrid had hoped it would be, because Mormor had wired some of her savings to a Nigerian prince. But when Astrid sold the house a year after Mormor's death, we had enough to put a down payment on a brand-new apartment in Kitsilano, on the west side of Vancouver.

Even though I missed Mormor, I loved our new place. It was small, but it was ours. The chemical aroma of fresh carpet was still in the air. Everything sparkled with newness. Astrid hung her bold canvases everywhere. We ate my favourite foods for supper, like cheese on toast with pickles and fish fingers with peas.

I started third grade at Waterloo Public School, and soon I had not just a friend, but a best friend. Dylan Brinkerhoff and I hung out all the time, playing with Lego and reading books like *Ripley's Believe It or Not!* and *Grossology*. We even made a magazine called *Stories from Ur Anus!* and wrote articles about UFO sightings and poltergeists. Astrid got another job, answering phones at a TV production company. And Emily Carr, where she still taught two nights a week, was just a short bus ride away.

But a year and a half after we moved in, two things happened.

Number one: Astrid lost both her jobs. It wasn't anything she'd done, not this time. Her evening class didn't get enough enrollment for another semester, so it was cancelled. And the production company went bankrupt.

Number two: Our building started to sink.

Yes. Sink.

It had been built on top of what used to be a riverbed.

The apartment owners were on the hook for the repairs, which were going to cost forty thousand dollars. *Each.*

We didn't have forty thousand dollars. We clung to the place for another year. But finally Astrid had to sell it, at a loss.

The Two-Bedroom Rental

Really it was a one-bedroom plus den. We could hear our neighbours fighting and the carpet smelled funky, but overall it wasn't too bad. It was on the east side, near Commercial Drive, which meant I had to switch schools in the middle of the year. I didn't make any close friends, but on the plus side, I didn't make any enemies, either.

I missed Dylan a lot. We had a few visits, but Astrid didn't own a car and I was too young to take the bus alone. That meant Dylan's parents had to do all the driving, and they had two other kids with busy schedules. After a few months, we lost touch.

Astrid couldn't find any office or teaching work, so she got her first-ever waitressing job on the Drive. I had to spend quite a few evenings on my own. But I had my imagination and my library books, and I watched some of the shows Mormor and I used to enjoy together, like *Who, What, Where, When.*

One night Astrid came home early. She was fuming. 'This customer kept trying to feel my butt.' (Astrid has always

11

been a firm believer in talking to me like an equal.) 'Yet I'm the one who gets punished. Just because I threw a drink in his face so he'd stop.' That's when I understood she'd been fired.

We fell behind on the rent. But lucky for us, Astrid became friends with Yuri, the building's superintendent, and he cut us some slack. A few times a week she would make me dinner, then go downstairs to his apartment for a couple of hours. I guess he was her sort-of boyfriend, even if he never took her out on a proper date.

Then Astrid met Abelard.

She stopped visiting Yuri's apartment. I guess Yuri felt hurt, because he stuck an eviction notice on our door.

The One-Bedroom Basement

We moved again, further east, close to Boundary Road. That meant another new school. It was harder this time. Most of the other kids had been together since kindergarten; they didn't need a new friend.

'What the heck is in *your* gene pool?' a tall, pinched-looking girl named Marsha asked me one day.

'Fifty per cent Swedish, twenty-five per cent Haitian, twenty-five per cent French,' I replied. 'Add it up and it equals one hundred per cent Canadian.'

She pursed her lips. 'You look like a clown.'

It wasn't the first time someone had made fun of my hair.

When I was younger I'd wanted my mom to cut it all off, but she'd refused. Now I'm glad she did. It's part of who I am. I'm like Samson, before he met Delilah: it's my super-power. And Astrid loves my hair; she says it reminds her of two of her favourite singers, K'naan and Art Garfunkel. She says it's good to have a distinct feature, and most of the time I agree. So I put up with idiots like Marsha, right up to the end of sixth grade. But I didn't like that school. I didn't like our basement apartment, either. It smelled musty, and even on sunny days it was dark. Plus Abelard was there all the time.

Astrid managed to get another office job, at BC Hydro. But that one didn't last either. She told me they laid some people off, and since she was last in, she was first out. But from stuff I overheard, I think it was more than that; I think she got lippy with her supervisor. 'I don't suffer fools gladly,' I heard her say to Abelard, 'and that guy was *such* a fool.'

Two weeks after that, Abelard broke up with her. Which brings me to:

The Westfalia

The van belonged to Abelard.

My mom met him at a day-long meditation retreat. He was the instructor, or guru.

Astrid is still pretty even though she is forty-four. She's tall and slender and has long, wavy blonde hair. I've seen

13

men's heads turn when she walks down the street. So even though Abelard was ten years younger, he asked my mom out for coffee after the retreat, and from that moment on, they were inseparable. When we moved to the basement apartment, he pretty much moved in, too, parking his Westfalia out front.

Abelard reminded me of Jesus, but only in looks. He had long brown hair, a hipster beard and a moustache. He said he was a Buddhist, and he blathered on a lot about peace and love and tolerance, which would have been fine if he wasn't such a dink. First of all, he mooched off my mom, even though it was obvious that we barely had enough to make ends meet. And second of all, he had a temper. He'd swear at my mom because she threw his yoga pants in the dryer instead of letting them drip-dry, or because she'd accidentally interrupted one of his meditation sessions.

He was an Angry Buddhist.

I couldn't stand him.

One night in July, Abelard told Astrid that he was heading to India on a 'spiritual journey', and he couldn't be 'tethered' to her any more. They fought. I left the apartment and walked around the block ten times. On the one hand, I felt bad for Astrid, because I knew she liked Abelard. On the other hand, I was relieved. She deserved so much better.

By the time I returned, Abelard was gone.

But his Westfalia wasn't. It was still in the driveway. Astrid told me Abelard had gifted it to her, his small way of thanking her for being such a freeloader.

Now I'm finding out that Abelard has accused her of stealing the van.

I know my mom sometimes embellishes the truth. But any thinking person would be nuts to take Abelard at his word, because the guy is a snake. My best guess is that the truth lies somewhere in the middle.

But I'm getting ahead of myself.

A week after Abelard left for India, the landlord changed our locks. He'd been trying to get us out for a while because we were behind on the rent. We came home to find our belongings stacked on the front lawn. My gerbil, Horatio, sat on top of the pile, in his cage.

Horatio had been my tenth birthday present. I'd really wanted a dog, so at first I was disappointed when Astrid gave me a rodent. But when I looked into his beady little eyes and petted his soft black and white fur, I fell in love. Even though he couldn't fetch, or run, or do tricks, even though he had a brain the size of a peanut, I adored him. So when I saw him perched precariously on top of our stuff, I lost it. What if his cage had fallen and he'd been hurt? What if the door hadn't been securely fastened and he'd escaped? What if a hungry dog had come along? Horatio didn't *look* traumatised, but then again, it's hard to read complex emotions on a gerbil's face.

I started to cry. Loudly. Astrid wrapped me in a hug. 'It's OK, Lilla Gubben. It's OK.' (Lilla Gubben is one of her pet names for me; it means 'little old man' in Swedish. Apparently, when I was born, that's exactly what I looked like: bald and wrinkly.)

'How is it OK?' I wailed. 'We have nowhere to live!'

She gripped my shoulders and made me look at her. 'Don't you worry. I will figure something out. I always do.' And that brings me to:

Soleil's House

Astrid started phoning her friends to see if someone could put us up for a few nights.

Something my P.O.O. has taught me over the years is that my mom is really good at making friends, and even better at losing them. So I wasn't super surprised when Ingrid said no. Or when Karen hung up on her.

Astrid thought for a moment. Then she said, 'I'll try Soleil.'

Soleil was one of Astrid's students in her painting class at Emily Carr, and a fellow mom. They'd become fast friends. Then, two years ago, they had a huge fight.

I heard the whole thing from my bedroom. It started out as a celebration because Soleil had sold another painting, this time for a record sum. But after they'd finished a second bottle of wine, Astrid started talking about the mediocrity of the masses, and how she couldn't understand why boring, bland work like Soleil's was selling while her superior abstracts weren't. Soleil left in tears and they didn't speak again.

Until now.

'She says we can stay with her for a bit,' Astrid said when she got off the phone.

She looked just as surprised as I did.

We packed everything into the Westfalia and drove to Soleil's new house near Main Street and King Edward. She was waiting for us in the driveway of a big modern home when we pulled up. Astrid whistled quietly. 'Someone's moved up in the world.'

Soleil smiled when she saw me. She's tall and broad-shouldered and has a friendly face. 'Felix, you've grown so much.' Then she gave my mom a lukewarm hug. 'Astrid. How are you? What happened?'

'Last-minute "renoviction" by a scumbag landlord.' I almost had to admire how effortlessly the lies rolled off her tongue.

Soleil helped us carry everything into a bright, spacious basement. A painting of yellow roses hung on one wall.

'I remember that,' said Astrid. 'You painted it at Emily Carr.'

'And you told me it was "technically fine, but emotionally dead". You didn't think I was living up to my full potential.'

Astrid's silence filled the room.

I watched Soleil's pale skin turn bright pink. 'My rose paintings have become my bestsellers. I can't seem to keep up with demand.'

My P.O.O. told me we were heading into dangerous territory. 'Would you like to pet my gerbil—' I asked, but Astrid spoke before Soleil could answer.

'I'm happy for you, Soleil, I really am.' I breathed a sigh of relief. Until she added, 'Your work is perfect for corporate lobbies and boardrooms.'

Oh boy.

Soleil wound her arms tightly across her chest. 'Arpad's parents are arriving at the end of the week. But you're welcome to stay until then.'

'You didn't mention that before,' Astrid said.

'I'm mentioning it now,' said Soleil, her gaze fixed on the yellow roses.

Soleil and her family had plans for the evening, so Astrid and I walked over to Helen's Grill and ordered the all-day breakfast for supper. I felt anxious. Not having a place to live can do that to a person.

The waitress brought us our plates. 'Why do breakfast foods always taste better at dinner?' Astrid asked.

'It's a scientific mystery.'

We ate in silence for a while. Then Astrid said, 'I have a fun idea.'

I looked at her, my mouth full of scrambled eggs.

'We'll live in the van. Just for a few weeks, until I find us another place. Think about it, Felix. It'll be the ultimate summer vacation. The freedom, the adventure . . . My favourite book when I was nineteen was *On the Road,* by Jack Kerouac. It'll be a blast.'

I thought about it. The furthest I'd ever travelled was to Victoria; my entire class had visited the provincial parliament buildings when I was ten. Marsha had pulled my hair on the bus, the whole way there and the whole way back. 'Could we travel? Go across BC? Or maybe as far as the Rockies?'

'Of course.'

'Can we afford it?'

'For a month, yes. I have some savings.'

'If you have savings, why did we fall behind on the rent?'

Astrid popped a strip of bacon into her mouth. 'The landlord was gouging us. The number of times I asked him to repair things that never got fixed . . . He *owed* us a few months rent-free for the crap we put up with.'

'Oh.'

'So, what do you say? Ultimate summer vacation?'

I wasn't convinced. But I didn't want to be a party pooper. 'I guess so. Sure.' We high-fived to seal the deal.

And that brings me to the beginning of August.

To the day we started living in a van.

AUGUST

The Volkswagen Westfalia is not a soccer-mom van, or a delivery van, or a minivan. It is in a class of its own.

Ours – and I *will* continue to call it ours for now – is a Vanagon Syncro, circa 1987, in gunmetal grey. It has a pop-up roof for extra sleeping space, and a built-in awning, which is brilliant for sitting outside in the summer. There is a two-ring stove that runs on a propane tank, a sink with a pump that leads to a huge plastic container of water so you can cook and wash dishes, and a bar-sized fridge. It has a table that can be lowered for meals and games. The back-seat pulls out, creating a big bed. Once the top is popped up, you can open another bed 'upstairs'.

It also has little cubbyholes for storage tucked into every available nook and cranny. It was designed to use every square inch to its maximum potential.

In short, the Westfalia is a masterpiece.

But I'm pretty sure it's only meant to be lived in temporarily, for vacations and such. And at first, that was all Astrid and I had in mind.

'We have to pack light,' she said to me after our first of two sleepless nights in Soleil's basement.

We started to sift through our belongings, deciding what to bring and what to leave behind. It was a brainteaser, because even though the Westfalia uses every square inch well, there are not that many square inches to begin with.

So Astrid and I came up with two important questions: *Is this something I use every day?* If the answer was yes, it went into the van. Things like:

Plates, bowls, cutlery, glasses and mugs – two sets of each

One pot, one frying pan, plus a few more cooking utensils

Dish soap, dishrags

Shampoo, deodorant, toothbrushes, toothpaste

First-aid kit

Flashlights, headlamps

Two sets of sheets, pillows, sleeping bags and towels

Clothes – enough for one week

Once we had our essentials, we asked the second question: *Is this something I feel I can't live without?* For Astrid, those items were a small stack of books, our Trivial Pursuit game, and her drawing pencils, paints, easel and sketchbooks. For me, it was Horatio, a few DK Eyewitness books, my dog-eared copy of *Tales from Moominvalley* and Mel.

Astrid wrinkled her nose at my *tomte*. 'Does that really need to come with us?' My mom has never liked Mel; she says she finds his gaze disconcerting.

'Yes,' I replied. If the Westfalia was going to be our temporary home, I figured we needed all the protection we could get.

Next we borrowed some cleaning supplies from Soleil and gave the van a good scrub. Abelard had left a few things behind, including a tool kit, a Patagonia rain jacket, a space heater and a sandwich bag full of marijuana. Astrid kept the tool kit and the space heater and gave me the rain jacket. I don't know what happened to the bag of marijuana, and that is the honest truth.

After our second night in Soleil's basement, we loaded up the Westfalia. Soleil's twins came out to watch before their dad, Arpad, drove them to their Mechatronics camp.

When we were done, we looked for Soleil in the garage, which had been converted into her studio. She was working on another rose painting, pink ones this time.

'Well, we're off on our road trip,' Astrid said.

'What about the rest of your things?'

'If it's all right with you, we'll leave them here. Just till the end of the month.' Astrid put a hand on my head, and I knew that was my cue to give Soleil a winning smile.

Soleil's eyebrows knit together. 'OK. But just till then.'

'Thanks for letting us stay,' I said, since it seemed my mom wasn't going to.

Soleil put down her paintbrush and gave me a hug. 'It was nice to see you again, Felix. You take care of yourself.'

She didn't look at Astrid. She just turned back to her painting without another word.

Astrid was right. Living in the Westfalia for the month of August *was* a blast, once I got over the initial disappointment that we wouldn't get to travel much. Astrid figured that out the first time we had to fill up the tank with gas. It cost, as Astrid said, *an arm and a leg*. 'I'm sorry, Böna.' This is another of her nicknames for me; it means 'bean' in Swedish. 'But think of all the beautiful places we can visit in and around Vancouver! Grouse Mountain, Stanley Park, Wreck Beach—'

'Not Wreck Beach!' Wreck Beach is famous for being 'clothing optional'. Astrid used to take me there when I was little. It was fine when I was five, but now that I was twelve and a half, you couldn't pay me enough to go.

'Fine. Prude. I'm just saying, there are lots of great places.'

And there were. We stayed in Stanley Park. We treated ourselves to a drive up Highway 99, and paid for camping at Alice Lake. We stayed in Lighthouse Park. Nobody bothered us. It really was like having a long summer vacation right in our own city. We spent our days swimming, hiking and reading. We were seldom far from a library. I read books like *A Short History of Progress* and *A Little History of the World,* and classics like *Great Expectations*. Astrid set up her easel outside and painted. The nights were warm, and we hooked the mesh tarp to the back of the van to let in air but not bugs. I could look through the skylight from my upper bunk to the stars.

Even though the only degree Astrid ever got is from the Ontario College of Art and Design, she is highly educated; before she landed at OCAD, she was in university for five years and switched her major three times. As she puts it, she knows 'a little about a lot'. She taught me how to find the zodiac signs in the sky. She told me stories from Roman, Greek and Norse mythology. I learned about Odin and Thor, and Venus and Neptune and Zeus and Apollo.

There was no Abelard. No angry landlord. No school. No Marsha.

It was wonderful.

Dare I say it was even a little bit magical?

Because it was so magical, we put off thinking about the future. Astrid sent her résumé out to lots of companies to try to get another office job, and she contacted Emily Carr, but no one was hiring. She didn't seem worried; we had savings, enough to tide us over for a while. We looked at a few apartments, but most landlords wanted current pay stubs.

One landlord leered at Astrid and told her he didn't need

any pay stubs or references. But the basement apartment was as creepy as he was.

'I prefer the van,' she said.

'Me too,' I agreed.

But as August crept to a close and the days grew shorter, we knew we had some decisions to make.

'Felix,' she said one evening as we set up our Trivial Pursuit board outside, 'we may need to stick it out in the van, just for one more month. Until I get a job.'

'It's OK.' And really, at the time, it was.

'You know what's great about this?'

'What?'

'You can register at any public school you want for seventh grade.' This was good news. My last two schools hadn't been terrible, but they hadn't been great, either. I'd felt a constant, low-grade loneliness.

'How about Blenheim? They have a late French immersion programme that starts in seventh grade. I've always wanted to learn French.' I didn't add that it was partly because of my dad. 'Plus it's in Kitsilano.' My fondest school memories were from our time in Kits.

Astrid's eyes lit up. 'That would be perfect for you. *Et nous pouvons parler en français ensemble.*' Astrid also knew French; it was yet another subject she had studied in university.

But then I remembered something my old friend Dylan had told me. 'Blenheim is the *only* late French immersion programme on the west side,' I said.

'So?'

'So, it's mostly an English-speaking school. They only have two classrooms for the French stream. Which means space for about sixty kids. And it's first come, first served. Dylan's sister got in, but she applied months in advance.'

Astrid thought for a moment. 'Don't despair. We'll go there tomorrow. And Felix?' She looked me in the eye. 'Let me do the talking.'

Astrid's Guidebook to Lies

I suppose I need to pause here to explain that yes, on occasion, my mother lies. But it's important to note that she has *levels* of lies, and rules surrounding each. Sort of like the Church of Scientology and their levels of Operating Thetans, her rationales don't always make a lot of sense. But this is how I break them down in my head.

The Invisible Lie

This is your run-of-the-mill white lie, the type we all tell multiple times a day without even thinking about it. For example, say you've just been diagnosed with a terminal illness and your waiter/bus driver says, 'How are you?' And you say, 'Fine.' Because it's understood that they don't want to know the truth. They're just being polite. And you don't feel like telling a stranger anyway. You both want to move on with your day.

The 'Give Peace a Chance' Lie

We all tell this sort of lie, to spare someone's feelings. An example: a couple of years ago, Astrid's waitress friend Gina asked, 'Does my butt look big in these jeans?'

Now. Gina is a large woman, with a butt to match. So, yes, her butt looked big in those jeans. But Astrid didn't miss a beat. She answered with an emphatic, 'No.' When I called her on it later, she said, 'Ask yourself this, Felix: what good would come of me telling her yes? She already worries about her weight. I don't need to add to her self-esteem issues.'

'But you're her friend. Shouldn't friends tell each other the truth?'

'Sometimes people don't want honesty; they want a little comfort. Besides, her butt looked no bigger in those jeans than they did in any of her other jeans. And it's a perfectly good-looking butt, a very proportional butt. So technically I wasn't lying.'

The 'Embellishment' Lie

Astrid would argue that embellishing isn't lying, it's just adding some flavour, like putting more spices into a dish. For example, she will pad her résumé with things that aren't, shall we say, *accurate,* depending on the type of job she's applying for. When she was first looking for restaurant work, she wrote that she had 'extensive experience in the service industry'.

'Since when?' I asked when I read it.

'Since you were born. I've been waiting on you hand and foot ever since.'

The 'No One Gets Hurt' Lie

These are bald-faced lies aimed at helping out the liar in some way. But – and this is crucial – they *harm no one*.

This type of lie will become clearer in a moment.

And lastly, there is:

The 'Someone Might Lose an Eye' Lie

These are the worst types of lies, the kind that have the potential to hurt the teller, or the tellee, or both.

Astrid doesn't tell these often, and when she does, I don't think she does it on purpose. For example, I don't think she meant to lie when she told her friend Ingrid she'd pay her back the five hundred dollars she borrowed. Or when she told her friend Karen the same thing. I think she believed she would pay them back. But she didn't. She didn't return Ingrid's expensive make-up kit, either. They felt hurt, and used, and eventually they cut her out of their lives. Which was a bummer, because Ingrid's daughter Violet had been my favourite babysitter. But once Ingrid vanished from our lives, so did Violet.

Come to think of it, my mom has pushed a lot of people

away with this type of lie. Including Daniel, the man who happens to be my dad.

Anyway. I just needed to explain these categories before I continue with the story. Because Astrid is about to tell a No One Gets Hurt and a Someone Might Lose an Eye, all in one day.

SEPTEMBER

'Hi, I'm Astrid Knutsson, and this is my son, Felix.' We were in the office of Blenheim Public School. Astrid had worn her prettiest peasant blouse and put on lipstick. 'We sent in our registration forms for the French immersion programme back in the spring, and we've been out of the country all summer.'

The secretary was at his computer behind the counter, playing solitaire. He shut down the game and opened a folder. 'Can you spell the last name, please?'

'K-N-U-T-S-S-O-N. I was surprised there wasn't any paperwork waiting for us when we got back last night, so we thought we'd just pop in.' She smiled. She has a radiant smile.

The secretary's brow furrowed. 'We have no record of receiving his registration form.'

'Oh, it must be there. It was probably one of the first you received, if that's any help.'

This time he got up and moved to a filing cabinet. He sifted through a folder once, twice. 'I don't know what to tell you. It isn't here.'

'I don't understand. It must be there. We intentionally applied early. Felix has been dreaming of this for the past two years.'

'Dreaming,' I echoed. I added a tremor to my voice, which I personally thought was a nice touch.

He shrugged helplessly. 'Mrs Knutsson—'

'*Ms,*' she corrected. 'Single parent. What's your name?'

'Obasi.'

'Obasi, there has to be a mistake. Perhaps someone misplaced it on this end?'

Obasi bristled at this suggestion. 'The only person on this end is me.'

'Well, then, that's an impossibility,' Astrid said quickly.

'Except,' Obasi said. 'A temp did fill in when I was sick in late March.'

'That's exactly when we sent it in!' Honestly, Astrid is very quick on her feet. She turned to me. 'Oh goodness. Felix, I'm so sorry.'

'But – this is all I've wanted. For years.' I actually managed to tear up a little, for real. *Je veux learnay le français,*' I added for effect.

Astrid held me close. Her voice was wobbly when she said, 'This is all my fault. I should have made a copy of the forms. I should have checked that they'd been received.'

'Now, now,' said the secretary. 'Don't blame yourself.'

'Are you a parent, Obasi?'

'Not yet. But my husband and I are trying to adopt.'

'That's so wonderful. You'll be able to share parenting responsibilities. I won't lie, it's hard doing it all on your own. And now I've really messed up.'

'You didn't do anything wrong. It was probably that darned temp.'

Astrid had him on the hook. Now all she needed to do was reel him in. 'Isn't there anything we could do?'

Obasi glanced around and lowered his voice. 'I shouldn't do this, but . . . a spot did open up just this morning. Normally I'm supposed to go to the waiting list . . . but seeing as you sent in your form ages ago . . .'

'You would really do that?' said Astrid.

Obasi nodded. I pulled away from Astrid's embrace. 'Thank you!' I said. 'Thank you, thank you, you've made me the happiest boy on earth! God bless us, every one!' I'm not sure why I quoted Tiny Tim from *A Christmas Carol*, but Astrid clearly thought it was over the top, because she elbowed me in the ribs.

Obasi slid some forms across the counter. 'Fill these out.'

Astrid gave him another dazzling smile. 'Obasi, you just did your good deed of the year. Thank you so much.'

He smiled back at her. 'It has to be our little secret.'

'Oh, definitely.'

I sat beside Astrid as she filled out the forms. I noticed that under *Parent or Guardian*, she put her information and hers alone.

When she reached *Address*, she paused. She glanced at Obasi, who was absorbed in a new game of solitaire. Then she pointed at the page. I read what it said: *Address must be in west side catchment. Please provide proof of residence in form of government-issued ID or a phone or hydro bill.*

This was a stumbling block. So far she'd had our mail forwarded from our old address to a post office box in East Vancouver, not in the catchment area.

Astrid stood up. 'Obasi, I clearly haven't had my morning coffee yet. I've forgotten some pertinent information at home. Here are all the other forms. I beg you, do not give up that spot. We'll be back first thing in the morning with everything else.'

He frowned. 'I can hold it till ten a.m. tomorrow, but that's it.'

'Not a problem.' She flashed him her smile one last time.

Back in the van, she sat in the driver's seat, silent. I knew to stay quiet; I knew she was figuring out what to do next.

After a few minutes she turned the key in the ignition. 'No worries. I've got it.'

We waited until six o'clock that night. 'I need to be sure he's home from work,' Astrid said. She didn't elaborate on who 'he' was.

At 6:01 sharp we drove up to a house in Kitsilano. There were bikes and a trampoline out front. 'Hey,' I said. 'This is

Caitlin's house.' I'd gone to school with her, back when we'd owned our apartment. 'Why are we—'

Astrid just held up a hand and hopped out of the van. 'Wait here.'

I watched as she walked up to the front door and knocked. Caitlin's dad, Mr Poplowski, answered the door.

I swear he looked taken aback when he saw my mom. He closed the door behind him and stepped onto the porch, like he didn't want anyone else in his family to see.

They talked for a bit. He seemed agitated. Then he went back inside. Astrid turned and gave me the thumbs-up. Unlike Mr Poplowski, she looked perfectly relaxed.

A few minutes later, the door opened again. Mr Poplowski handed my mom some papers. Then he slammed the door.

Astrid practically bounced back to the van. 'There. That's taken care of.'

'What did you do?'

'We needed an address. He provided me with one.'

'We're going to give the school Caitlin's address?'

She laughed. 'No, no. Her dad's letting us use his law office address, which is on Broadway. Offices on the main floor, apartments upstairs, but the school will never know the difference. We can have all our mail redirected there.'

'And he's OK with that?'

She pulled away from the curb, smiling. 'He has no choice.'

'But why—'

'Felix. Enough questions.'

I shut up. But I was thinking about the last time I'd seen Mr Poplowski.

It was winter. We were living in our apartment. I'd gone to school feeling fine, but mid-morning I'd suddenly thrown up. The school nurse said I was coming down with the flu. She called my mom a couple of times, but there was no answer, so she told me to lie down on the cot in her office. After a while I got bored. When the nurse went to the toilet, I slipped out; I figured I'd walk home and lie down there, because at least we had a TV.

I let myself in to our apartment. My mom was there – with Mr Poplowski. He was putting on his shoes. 'Hey, Felix, my man! What are you doing home?' He sounded overly enthusiastic.

'Caitlin's dad is a lawyer,' my mom said. 'He was helping me look over the apartment contract.'

I was feeling woozy, plus I was only eight or nine, so I didn't question it. But my P.O.O. told me it was odd for my mom to have a business meeting in her dressing gown.

I don't want to think too much about all that. But I'm guessing Caitlin's dad figured it was better to participate in a small lie than to have a bigger lie exposed.

We drove straight to the Kits library. Astrid took out one

of the papers Caitlin's dad had given her: a hydro bill for his law office. She fired up a library computer and found a font that matched the hydro bill. She typed in her name, *Astrid Knutsson,* and printed it out. Then she carefully cut it out and pasted it over Mr Poplowski's name. She photocopied the bill and showed me the results.

It looked good. Real.

We walked into the office the next morning at 9:01 sharp. 'Ah, perfect,' Obasi said. 'You're here.' Astrid handed him the bill, and he studied it. 'We don't normally accept photocopies. We like to have the original.'

'The originals are with my accountant at the moment.'

'That's fine. Just bring one in when you can.' Obasi smiled at me and held out his hand. We shook. 'Congratulations, Felix. We'll see you next week.'

I felt happy – giddy, even – as we climbed back into the van. August had been fun, but I was looking forward to being around people my own age again, maybe even making a friend or two.

Astrid didn't turn on the ignition. 'Just so we're clear, Felix. When you start school, it would be best not to tell any of your classmates about this.'

'About how you got me into the programme?'

'No. Well, yes. That, too. But about our living arrangements.' She indicated the van. 'You know, and I know, it's strictly temporary. But other people . . . they might not understand. We don't want to give anyone a reason to call the MCFD.'

A chill seized my heart.

MCFD. Ministry of Children and Family Development.

We'd had one run-in with them, back in April. Astrid and Abelard had had one of their more spectacular fights the night before. A social worker showed up at the door the next day with a pile of questions. It was probably our landlord who'd called them, because he lived upstairs. Maybe he was worried I was being physically abused. I wasn't.

Abelard never laid a hand on *me*.

Anyway. I knew from that experience, and from stories my mom had told me, that you did not want to get on the MCFD's radar. No way, no how. So I said, 'OK.'

Not talking about my living arrangements didn't seem like a big deal at the time.

Like Astrid said, this was temporary.

We'd have a place to live in no time.

I was diarrhoea-nervous on my first day at Blenheim, which isn't good at the best of times, and *really* isn't good when you're living in a van.

Luckily we'd spent that night parked a few blocks from the school, across from the local community centre. Astrid had planned it that way so we'd have a place to freshen up in the morning. I dashed over to use their toilet three times in half an hour.

The day before, we'd driven to Soleil's house to collect more of our things; some thicker sweaters, warmer jackets and shoes, and the school supplies I had from last year. The driveway was empty when we arrived, and all the blinds were drawn.

'I don't think anyone's home,' I said.

'Not a problem.' Astrid pulled away. I thought we were leaving. Instead she made two right-hand turns and stopped in the alley, outside Soleil's back gate.

My intestines clenched. 'What are you doing?'

'Going inside.'

'Mom,' I said. She looked at me sharply; she doesn't like me calling her that. 'We are not breaking in.'

'Who said anything about breaking in?' She pulled a key from her pocket.

'Soleil gave you a key?' I asked as we climbed out of the van.

Astrid opened the back gate. 'Yes and no. She gave it to me for our stay. I had a copy made before I gave it back.'

My intestines re-clenched. 'Then we *are* breaking in.'

She inserted the key into the door. 'Not if we're only taking our own things.'

I started to hiccup. This happens when I get anxious. 'What if they come home?'

'They won't. They're away on vacation. I did my research.'

'So you planned it this way. *Hic!*'

Astrid pushed the door open. We were greeted by a high-pitched whine.

An alarm system. My bowels loosened.

But Astrid just punched a code into the alarm pad and the high-pitched sound stopped. 'Böna, it's OK. Soleil will never know we were here.'

We wound up spending the entire afternoon there. Astrid did all our laundry. Then, in the guest washroom, she filled a bath with bubbles for me. My reluctance melted away when I got into that tub. It was glorious. While I was soaking and shampooing, she filled the Jacuzzi tub in the master bathroom for herself.

I'm kind of ashamed to admit this now, but we also raided their freezer. A frozen lasagne was calling out to us.

So we cooked it and ate it. Astrid found a plastic container in one of Soleil's drawers and put in the leftovers for me to take for lunch.

It was actually pretty awesome, being inside a real house for the first time in a month. So after dinner we still didn't leave. We sat in the family room and watched TV, including *Who, What, Where, When*, my favourite. It's like *Jeopardy!* on steroids. Unlike Alex Trebek, the host of *Who, What, Where, When*, Horatio Blass, waves his arms and speaks in a booming voice and says, 'Wooooo-hooooo!' a lot.

I shouted out the answers before the contestants. I was almost always right. This is not a brag; it is simply that I have a strange knack for storing facts. And since my mom has studied everything from anthropology to world history to English literature, I've picked up a truckload of facts over the years. 'You are a sponge,' a teacher said to me once after I'd quoted, from memory, Martin Luther King Jr's 'I Have a Dream' speech.

While we watched TV, my gaze drifted to an enormous black and white family portrait that hung above the fireplace. Soleil, her husband and their twin sons were wearing almost identical outfits; off-white crewneck sweaters and dark trousers.

I felt a twinge of envy, I will not deny it. They looked so happy. So rich.

We didn't want to draw attention by putting on the lights, so we left as darkness started to fall.

I feel it's important to mention that we left the place spotless. Cleaner, perhaps, than it had been when we arrived. And all we took was the lasagne. And the plastic container. And a beer for Astrid and a soda for me.

I'm pretty sure it was simply a strange coincidence when, a week later, my mom was wearing a sweater I hadn't seen before.

Off-white. Crewneck.

Astrid gave me a final once-over before I left for school. My hair was, as always, a massive pouf of blond, and it was silky clean and smelled magnificent. I wore jeans, bought at Value Village – why anyone shops anywhere else is beyond me – and my favourite T-shirt, which had a Canadian flag on it and the words MEMBER OF THE 'EH' TEAM.

'You look great,' Astrid said. 'I hope it's a wonderful day.'

'Same to you.' She was going job hunting. She wore a pair of smart grey trousers, ballet flats and one of her pretty blouses. Astrid knows how to make a good first impression. It's the later impressions that are sometimes a problem.

I walked the few blocks to Blenheim. It was a beautiful day. Chestnut trees lined either side of the street, their leaves rustling in the breeze. My stomach burbled because I'd only eaten a banana for breakfast; I was too nervous for anything more.

When I walked through the front doors of the old

yellow-brick building, I tried to carry myself with a confidence I didn't feel.

My eyes just happened to land on a boy further down the hall. He looked like he'd gotten out of bed five minutes earlier. His striped T-shirt and jeans were wrinkled, he had a wicked case of bedhead, and he'd accidentally tucked his T-shirt into his pants.

I recognised him immediately.

It was Dylan Brinkerhoff, my old best friend.

'Dylan, hi,' I said, my voice cracking.

He turned around and looked at me blankly for a moment. My heart sank. Then his lips parted into a big grin, revealing a mouthful of metal. 'Felix!' He threw his arms around me and gave me a hug. 'Are you here for Late French Immersion?' He spoke with a slight lisp thanks to the braces, like they were pulling on his tongue.

'Yes. Please tell me you are, too.'

'I am! Does this mean you're back in the neighbourhood?'

'It does indeed.'

'That's so great! Where do you live?'

I blinked rapidly. I hadn't expected the question so soon. 'On the west side, but barely. Long bus ride.' I told myself it was an Invisible Lie.

'Who's your teacher?' he asked.

'Monsieur Thibault.'

'Same. What are the odds?' I was about to say the odds were pretty good since there were only two late immersion classes, but I didn't. 'Oh man, this is so awesome!'

I could not have agreed more.

Dylan and I found seats in the middle of the classroom. It felt like a safe place to start. I counted twenty-eight kids, an even split of boys and girls. There was none of the normal first-day chatter; most of us had come from different schools for the programme, so we were *all* new, which was, frankly, a relief.

A man walked into the room. He looked like he was maybe twenty-five, and he had big, thick arms and a broad chest. He sported a black beard and a carefully manicured handlebar moustache. And he had tattoos. Lots and lots of tattoos. '*Bonjour, je m'appelle Monsieur Thibault.* Hello, I'm Mister Thibault.'

Dylan and I glanced at each other. Monsieur Thibault looked more like a Hells Angel than a teacher.

He told us, in English, that he'd been born and raised in Quebec City, and that he had nine – nine! – brothers and sisters. He reminded us that we were all in the same boat, so there was no need to be nervous. My P.O.O. told me he was going to be great. 'For today and today only we will speak English. Starting tomorrow, everything will be *en français.* Now, let's go around the room and introduce ourselves. Tell us why you chose to be in this programme.'

He started at the back and worked his way up. When it

was Dylan's turn, he said, 'I'm Dylan Brinkerhoff. My older sisters, Cricket and Alberta, did this programme. They said I should do it, too. I guess that's why I'm here.'

I was next. 'I'm Felix Knutsson. I'm half Swedish, but I never learned much Swedish, and I'm a quarter Haitian and a quarter French, but I don't know Creole or French. And I like languages, and I like to challenge myself, so . . . here I am.'

Most of the introductions were like ours, short and in English. Then Monsieur Thibault got to the final student, who sat (predictably, in retrospect) in the front row.

Winnie Wu.

Winnie's long black hair was coiled into a French braid, which I only later realised was intentional (*French* braid. Get it?). She wore a white blouse and a plaid skirt with red knee socks and black leather shoes. Around her neck was a gold chain with two pendants; a jade heart, and a little gold cross. On her head, tilted artfully, was a red beret.

Je suis ici parce que j'aime toutes les choses françaises. J'ai acheté les "listening tapes" pour étudier.'

Silence. Most of us could barely count to ten in French; we had no idea what she'd just said. But Monsieur Thibault broke into a delighted grin. 'Excellent, Winnie—'

Winnie wasn't finished. *'Mes parents m'ont emmenée à Las Vegas l'hiver passé et j'ai vu la Tour Eiffel, et vraiment, ça a été l'amour au premier regard! Maintenant j'aime toutes les choses françaises – la cuisine, la culture, le cinéma. Quand nous aurons assez d'argent, nous irons visiter le vrai Paris. Et, un jour, je veux vivre en France.'*

Monsieur Thibault gave us the condensed version: 'Winnie became a devoted Francophile after seeing the Eiffel Tower.' Then he coughed. 'In Las Vegas.'

And it was like two years hadn't passed since I'd last seen Dylan because we looked at each other and cracked up; but in our special way, that only we could hear.

We spent the rest of the day playing games to get to know each other. When the final bell rang, Dylan asked, 'Want to come over?'

I wanted to so badly. But I was anxious to find out how my mom's day had gone. 'I can't today. How about tomorrow?'

'Sure.'

We walked together to our lockers. 'Hey, do you still have your poltergeist?' When I first met Dylan, he'd been convinced that their house had a friendly but mischievous poltergeist named Bernard, because his things were always going missing.

'Yes! I'm pretty sure he took a sock just this morning!'

I smiled. I loved that Dylan still believed in Bernard.

We said our goodbyes. I walked back to the van and did the special knock on the side. Astrid slid the door open. 'How was your first day?'

I told her all about my new school, and Dylan.

'That's wonderful, Felix.'

'How was yours?'

She smiled. 'I got a job. At a coffee shop in Kerrisdale. Bean There, Donut That. I said I had a lot of experience serving coffee, which is essentially true; I serve myself coffee every morning.'

We high-fived. 'Astrid, that's fantastic.'

'Pay isn't great, but it's lots of shifts, and I get to keep whatever goes in the tip jar. It'll do till something better comes along, and in the meantime we can start looking for a place. I'll be able to give a work reference and show my pay stub in a couple of weeks.'

We celebrated. Astrid heated up two cans of vegetarian chilli on the stove. I gave Horatio extra lettuce. We set up our collapsible lawn chairs in the park across the street and ate our chilli alfresco, along with some raw carrots and cucumber. We had apples and store-bought cookies for dessert.

By ten p.m. we were in our beds, reading by headlamp, when there was a tap on the van door.

Astrid sat bolt upright. 'Who is it?'

'Just a concerned neighbour,' said a man's voice. 'You guys have been parked here for a few nights in a row. Just wondering who you're visiting.'

'Our friends,' Astrid said smoothly. 'We sleep out here to give them space.'

'I see. Which house do your friends live in?'

'The flesh-pink one.' Flesh-pink houses were everywhere in this neighbourhood.

'The Woodbridges?'

'That's right.'

'OK. I'm just going to knock on their door to confirm.'

'Please do.'

I peeled back one of the curtains and watched him walk down the block. My mom climbed into the driver's seat. 'Sorry, Felix. We'll need to find a new spot for tonight.'

The man glanced up as we drove past.

Astrid gave him the one-finger salute.

I went to Dylan's house after school the next day, even though I was pretty pooped. After we'd found a new place to park the van, it had taken me a long time to unwind. I'd had to list all the United States in alphabetical order in my head, from Alabama to Wyoming, *and* go through the entire table of periodic elements, before I'd finally drifted off to sleep.

Still, I was excited as we walked the five blocks to his house. It had been a long time – I mean a *long* time – since I had been to a friend's place, since at my last couple of schools I'd been lacking the key ingredient (i.e., friends).

The Brinkerhoffs' home was exactly as I remembered it. The porch still looked like it was caving in. The neon-yellow paint was peeling. The grass was brown and patchy. There were old children's toys on the lawn, even though Dylan, the youngest, hadn't played with them in years. Inside, you could barely see the hardwood floors for the discarded shoes, socks, sweaters and books. They had dust bunnies that were bigger than Horatio. When I went into the kitchen there was a stack of dishes piled high in the sink that looked identical to the stack that had been there years earlier. My socks stuck a little bit to some spots on the floor, just like they had before.

It was wonderful. So full of life.

An enormous orange cat waddled into the kitchen and rubbed against Dylan's legs. 'This is Craig,' Dylan said as he scooped him up. 'He's two. We got him last year.' He held the cat out to me and I took him. Craig purred happily in my arms.

'Whoa. He must be eight kilos.'

'Nine.'

Dylan's older sister Alberta wandered in. She looked the same, too, with her long brown hair, lazy eye and unique T-shirt collection. This one read WHAT DOESN'T KILL YOU MAKES YOU STRONGER. EXCEPT FOR BEARS. BEARS WILL KILL YOU. 'Ooh, how sweet, Dylan's already made an ickle friend.' She took the milk out of the fridge and drank straight from the carton. 'Wait a sec. I'd recognise that hair anywhere. You're Bionicle Dork.'

I blushed just a little. 'That's me. But I prefer to be called Felix.'

'You guys used to run around in your *Toy Story* pyjamas with your Bionicles, making laser-gun sounds. *Pyoom pyoom pyoom!* Ha-ha-ha-ha-ha-ha-HEEE-haw!' Her laugh hadn't changed, either. 'You were adorable. Total nerd-bots.' She gave us both the once-over. 'Clearly some things haven't changed! Ha-ha-ha-ha-ha-ha-HEEE-haw!' Then she poured us both a glass of milk from the carton she'd just drunk from.

It was heaven.

You know how sometimes you don't realise how much you've missed something until you get it back? That's how I felt about having a friend again. It was like having blurry vision for a long time, then someone gives you a pair of glasses and you look at the world around you and go, 'Wow! *This* is what I've been missing!'

I went over to Dylan's house almost every day those first two weeks. He never asked to come to mine; his place was so close to school, it just made sense. We did our homework. He caught me up on all things Bernard. 'Just yesterday, OK? I left out *Settlers of Catan* on the coffee table cos me and Alberta were mid-game. I was winning. And this morning, all the pieces were moved around to make it seem like *she* was winning. I was all like, "Bernard, you sneaky rascal!"'

We also ate. A lot. Their cupboards were full of jumbo-sized items from Costco. We nuked pizza pops and burritos and stuffed our faces in front of the TV. Since I'd been eating most of my food out of cans for over a month, this was seriously the best.

One afternoon we caught a rerun of *Who, What, Where, When.* 'What iconic American novel includes the character of Becky Thatcher?' asked Horatio Blass.

'*The Adventures of Tom Sawyer*!' I shouted, a full three seconds before any of the contestants buzzed in.

'What was the name of Hitler's dog?'

'Blondi.'

'Who is the Greek god of wine?'

'Dionysus.'

At some point I realised that Dylan and Alberta – who'd wandered in from the kitchen – were staring at me. 'Wow. Egghead,' said Alberta.

Dylan threw a cushion at her. 'You're good, Felix. Really good.'

'Better even than my boyfriend, Henry,' said Alberta. 'And he's on the senior Reach for the Top team at our high school.'

'Alberta was on the junior team, but she was too dumb to make the senior,' Dylan explained.

Alberta threw the cushion back at him and left the room.

'You should apply to be a contestant,' said Dylan.

'I can't. You have to be at least eighteen.' Craig hopped onto the couch and sprawled out on his back between us, purring loudly.

'That's too bad. You could totally win!'

'I doubt that,' I said. 'But thanks.'

I always left before Dylan's parents came home. I liked the Brinkerhoffs, and I didn't want to have to answer questions about my mom and where we lived and maybe have to lie. Unlike some people I know, I am a terrible liar.

• • •

Astrid's job was going well. Sometimes I would walk all the way to the shop after I left Dylan's and stay until her shift ended. She would slip me a free hot chocolate, and if it wasn't busy, she'd have simple conversations with me in French. This was helpful, since we had to speak French in class all the time now. It was hard for everyone.

Except Winnie Wu.

Near the end of our second week, Monsieur Thibault broke us into pairs and assigned us each a picture book. We had to write a short paragraph about it in French.

'Felix, you'll be working with Winnie.'

I almost groaned out loud.

Winnie Wu was a royal pain in the *derrière*, to use the French word. She just could not stop talking. Or asking questions. About everything.

'Sir, have you eaten *escargots*? I tried them in Las Vegas Paris.'

'Sir, will we not also learn about *passé simple* at some point?'

'Sir, who decided which words would be feminine, *la*, and which words would be masculine, *le*?' She couldn't let the smallest thing go by without having something to say about it, all in irritatingly good self-taught French. My P.O.O. told me that she even got on Monsieur Thibault's nerves sometimes; when she'd asked her eighteenth question of the day, I'd see him inhale deeply, hold his breath for a few seconds, then exhale slowly.

And now I had to work with her.

Dylan grinned wickedly at me, showing off his hardware. *Good luck, sucker*, he mouthed.

I sat across from Winnie. She was wearing a different blouse with a different plaid skirt and her beret was green. I also noticed she had impeccable posture, straight white teeth and naturally red lips, *which never stopped moving.*

'We need to dig below the surface,' she said. 'We need to discuss the deeper implications faced by Walter, and his owners, as he goes through this particular plight. Are there, for example, some weightier themes at work that we haven't yet uncovered—'

'Oh my God!' I blurted in English. 'He's a *farting dog*!' The book we'd been assigned was *Walter le Chien qui Pète*.

'Felix, *en français, s'il vous plaît,*' Monsieur Thibault said.

Our 'paragraph' became two pages, single spaced. At least we got an A. But I told Dylan I would never, ever work with Winnie Wu again.

I made that vow on a Friday.

And broke it the following Monday.

'The school newspaper is looking for volunteers to write a few pages of the September edition in French,' Monsieur Thibault announced on Monday, at the beginning of our third week. 'It's published once a month. There's no extra credit, but it's a great way to work on your language skills. Anyone who's interested, we'll have our first meeting after school in room 222.'

'I think we should try it out,' Dylan said later in the cafeteria. He was eating a ham sandwich. His braces caught a lot of it, enough for an afternoon snack.

'Me too,' I replied.

'Remember that magazine we wrote when we were kids? *Stories from Ur Anus!?*'

'You wrote an article called "Aliens Probed My Butt!"'

'You wrote one called "Martian Steals All of Family's Pants!"'

We cracked up. Dylan sprayed a bit of his sandwich on me in the process, but I didn't mind; what's a bit of masticated food between friends?

• • •

After school we made our way to room 222. Monsieur Thibault was there with the editor of the paper, an eighth grader who introduced himself as Charlie Tuyen.

'Looks like you two are the only ones coming,' said Monsieur Thibault. 'So I guess we'll get started.'

'Thanks for being here,' Charlie began, just as the door opened and a latecomer arrived.

Winnie.

She looked flustered; her red beret was askew. 'Sorry I'm late,' she said. 'Donald thought it would be funny to steal my beret and use it as a Frisbee.' Donald was a kid in our class, and he seemed like kind of a jerk.

Winnie took the seat in front of me as Charlie continued. 'We want a French component to the paper, mostly for you guys in immersion, but also for the rest of the students who are doing regular French and want to practise their language skills. You can write about pretty much anything. We just need enough content to fill three pages.'

Winnie raised her hand.

'Yes?' said Charlie.

'That won't be a problem. Not for me, anyway.' Her red lips curled into a tiny, smug grin. Dylan and I looked at each other and fake-puked.

'OK, well, there's a crunch for the first issue, so if you could have stuff to me by Monday the thirtieth—'

Winnie raised her hand again.

'Yes?'

'I'm assuming you want hard-hitting stories? About politics, poverty, drugs?'

'Well, it's a school newspaper. It's meant to be pretty light and entertaining.'

Winnie's hand shot up again.

'You really don't need to keep raising your hand—'

'In other words, you want fluff,' she said, her lips pursed in disapproval.

Monsieur Thibault inhaled deeply. He exhaled slowly.

'Hey, write whatever you want,' said Charlie. 'I don't care. I just need it by the thirtieth. Meeting adjourned.' Charlie and Monsieur Thibault hightailed it out of the room.

'Let's go to my house,' Dylan said to me as we stood. 'Keep noodling ideas.'

Winnie turned to look at us. 'Excellent plan.'

Dylan and I shot each other a look that said *Crap*. Winnie must have seen, because her bottom lip started trembling. 'Oh. I get it. You didn't mean me.'

There was a long pause. 'You can come too if you want,' said Dylan, with zero enthusiasm.

This was where Winnie was supposed to grab a clue and say, 'No, it's OK.' Instead, her face lit up. 'Goody! I'll just go get my satchel.' She hurried out of the room.

I looked at Dylan. *'Goody?'*

'Satchel?'

It was going to be a long afternoon.

• • •

Winnie was just as annoying as we'd expected; possibly more so. First there was her expression when she entered Dylan's house. Her perfect red mouth became a little O of horror. She tried to cover. 'It's so . . . *charmant*.' She refused our offer of pizza pops and chips. 'Empty calories. Also, I could tell you all the reasons you should eat less meat for the sake of the planet—'

'Please don't,' said Dylan.

In the living room, she spread her jacket on the couch before she sat down. The couch was covered in cat hair, but still.

'So. Should we just toss out ideas?' asked Dylan.

Winnie took out a leather-bound notebook and a pen. 'I'll keep minutes.'

'I'll keep hours,' I said, chomping on a pizza pop.

'I'll keep seconds,' said Dylan, shovelling chips into his mouth.

Two out of three of us cracked up.

'I could do a crossword,' I said. 'And maybe an article on fun French facts. Like, stuff the French invented, or moments in history.'

'Great idea,' said Dylan.

'Where's the edge? Where's the journalistic rigour?' Winnie tapped her pencil on her notebook.

'Hey, I know,' said Dylan, ignoring her. 'I could write about poltergeists!'

'Perfect,' I said.

Winnie wrinkled her nose. 'Why would you do that?'

'Because they're cool and interesting,' said Dylan. 'Because we have one.'

'*Pfft*. Please. Poltergeists don't exist.'

'How do you know?' I asked, feeling defensive on Dylan's behalf. I had my own theories about Bernard, but I knew to keep them to myself.

'Because. Any thinking person knows that ghosts aren't real.'

Dylan started to make spluttering sounds. I pointed at the cross around her neck. 'Do you believe in God?'

'I do,' she said.

'So how is that any different?' asked Dylan. 'Have you *seen* God?'

'Have you *seen* your poltergeist?'

'No, but I've seen proof. He plays a ton of practical jokes. But he also looks out for us. Like, the other day, my sister slipped on the stairs, and this invisible force kept her from falling.'

Winnie opened her mouth to argue, but stopped herself. 'Fine. I can tell there's no use arguing with you two. Do your weird pseudo journalism. I'm going to write an investigative piece about asbestos. Our school was built a long time ago, meaning there's probably asbestos in the walls.'

Dylan looked at me. 'Sounds super,' he said.

'Super boring,' I added.

Again, two out of three of us cracked up.

As September drew to a close it got colder, especially at night. This is something you become acutely aware of when you live in a van.

But we adapted. As Astrid likes to say, living in a Westfalia definitely makes a person more resourceful. '*Resourceful*, Felix, is a good life skill to have.'

And we are nothing if not resourceful. Take Wi-Fi, for example. When we need it, we go to a coffee shop, or find an unsecured network. When something needs recharging, like a phone or batteries for our headlamps, we plug in somewhere like the Laundromat. Sometimes we plug in at a power source outside an empty house. On the west side of Vancouver, there are a lot of big, brand-new houses with no one living in them – Astrid says they are 'investment properties'. It's one of her pet peeves. 'Our city is becoming a playground for the rich. Enormous, empty homes, when so many people who live here can't find affordable housing. Our politicians should be ashamed of themselves,' she says. Over and over and over and over.

Astrid is very good at picking out which houses are

people-free. 'All the blinds drawn, check. Lights go on at the same time every night, check. Junk mail piles up, check. Sprinkler system on even if it's pouring rain, with zero consideration for water conservation, check.' It is surprisingly easy to pull up outside one of these houses as darkness falls and use their electricity. We fill up our water containers with their outdoor hoses at the same time. We've never broken in, unless you count—

But I'm getting ahead of myself.

We are also resourceful when it comes to food. A Westfalia kitchen is pint-sized. The tiny two-burner stovetop doesn't allow for elaborate meals, and we can't keep much stuff in the teensy fridge, so we eat a lot of stuff from cans. Pea soup, vegetarian chilli – my mom even lets me eat Chef Boyardee pasta once in a while, even though she says it is 'toxic waste'.

But to be clear, I am not malnourished; not too badly, anyway. I don't think I'm suffering from scurvy or a vitamin deficiency or anything like that. We shop at the No Frills, where you can get really good deals on produce they're about to throw out. And once in a while my mom will—

But I'm getting ahead of myself again.

I won't lie; some aspects of life in a Westfalia never get easier.

Like not having a bathroom. I miss that more than anything. We always try to stop for the night near a public restroom. We do our business in coffee shops, or McDonald's restaurants, which have nice facilities. We do a lot of armpit and bit-washing in sinks. Twice a week we go to a community centre and have long showers.

We do our best. But still. What I wouldn't give for a toilet to call my own.

There is also the lack of privacy. Two people, in a small space like that – I dare anyone to try it and not have it get on their nerves once in a while. It doesn't help that my mom snores like a trucker sometimes, even though she totally denies it.

And let's just say there are certain things an almost-thirteen-year-old would occasionally like to do, *private and very personal things*, that are impossible when the almost-thirteen-year-old's mother is sleeping three feet away.

That is all I will say about that.

But in September we were sure our living arrangements were temporary, so we managed. My mom moved the Westfalia every few nights so we wouldn't arouse suspicion. I secured Mel to the dashboard so he could watch over us. On the days we couldn't shower at a community centre I headed to school early and locked myself in the handicapped washroom, which was private and spacious. I kept a small toiletry kit in my locker with soap and deodorant, a spare toothbrush and toothpaste. I'd peel off my T-shirt and give my armpits a good, thorough wash. I'd scrub my face and brush my teeth and comb out my hair. And every time I was at Dylan's house, I would make sure to use his toilet to do a number two.

I told myself it wasn't gross.

I told myself it was *resourceful*.

And then came the day that I told Dylan and Winnie my first No One Gets Hurt.

It was Friday, and our articles were due on Monday, so we agreed to get together on the weekend to do final edits. 'We can't go to my place,' Dylan said. 'A bunch of our relatives are visiting from back east.' He looked at me. 'Could we go to yours?'

'I live pretty far.'

'That's OK,' said Winnie. 'We can bus.'

I opened and closed my mouth. Then I heard myself say, 'My mom's got the flu. Vomiting, diarrhoea – the works.'

Winnie's mouth formed that little O of horror. 'Well then, you can come to mine.' She gave me a stern look. 'But if you're contagious? I will murder you.'

Dylan and I took the bus together to Winnie's place on Saturday. It was in a brand-new eight-storey building at Fir Street and Seventh Avenue. She buzzed us up.

'Take off your shoes,' she whispered as she opened the door. She guided us down a narrow hallway into a small living room. It looked like something in an IKEA catalogue, only not as tidy. Sliding glass doors led to a balcony with views over the ocean and the North Shore Mountains. A pretty jade bird sat on the mantelpiece above a gas fireplace. 'Have a seat,' she whispered again.

'Is there a reason we're whispering?' I asked in a whisper, taking half of the love seat while Dylan took the other half.

'My mom's sleeping. She's an obstetrician. She delivered two babies last night.' Winnie said this with pride. 'Dad's a nurse. They met during a C-section fifteen years ago. Dad helped Mom pull the baby out. Pretty romantic, don't you think?'

Dylan made a face. 'Pretty gross.'

We went through our pieces one last time, arguing in whispers. 'Your articles are silly,' Winnie said.

'Your article is a snorefest.'

She ignored our comments, and we ignored hers. But we did let her correct our spelling and grammatical errors, because there were loads of them.

Mr Wu came in as we were finishing up. He was tall and skinny and had a friendly smile. His arms were weighed down with bags of groceries. 'Would your friends like some lunch?' he asked, also in a whisper. 'I just got back from T & T Supermarket.'

My stomach growled loudly in response. Astrid and I had eaten day-old doughnuts from her coffee shop for breakfast, but that was hours ago.

Winnie jumped up. 'I can make sandwiches with my homemade bread.'

Ten minutes later, the four of us were crowded into their

tiny kitchen, which was still twenty times bigger than the Westfalia's. Winnie served cheese sandwiches. 'You really made the bread?' I asked. It looked delicious.

She nodded. 'I started last year after I read an article about all the preservatives in store-bought. This one's gluten-free, with quinoa and chia seeds.'

I took a big bite and started to chew.

It took all my willpower not to spit it out. The bread tasted like sawdust and had the consistency of tree bark. I could tell from Dylan's face that he was struggling, too.

Winnie held out a plate to her dad. 'You sure you won't have one?'

Mr Wu patted his stomach. 'Wish I could. Still stuffed from a late breakfast. Honey, do you mind getting my water glass? I left it in the other room.'

The moment she was gone, he motioned to us. 'Quick. Take out the cheese and hand me the bread.' We did as we were told. We wolfed down the cheese while he slipped the bread into the garbage, making sure to put other items on top of it. When Winnie returned, he told a Give Peace a Chance. 'Your friends are bottomless pits! I'm making them lunch number two.' He started pulling stuff out of his grocery bags. 'Steamed pork buns, anyone?'

'*Bà*, what have I said about pork?' Winnie chastised.

'Once in a while I need my fix,' he said. I ate four of them. They were legit delicious.

Mr Wu seemed like a very good dad.

Before Dylan and I left, I used the bathroom. It was white and clean and smelled like lavender potpourri. They even had a heated toilet seat.

I sat there for a long time, feeling the warmth radiate through my bum. And suddenly, out of nowhere, tears pricked my eyes.

I longed for a toilet.

And I longed for my dad.

The first edition of the *Blenheim Bugle* came out on Wednesday. Monsieur Thibault gave us time to read it before lunch. It was eight pages, with the three French pages at the end. My article was featured first. I'll try to translate from memory. It went something like this:

Fun French Facts, Part 1
By Felix Knutsson

The French invented many things: The Braille system. Pasteurisation. Hot-air balloons. But I am going to tell you about a bloodier invention: the guillotine.

It was made by a doctor named Joseph-Ignace Guillotin in the late 1700s. He was against capital punishment. He made the guillotine because it was a nicer way to execute someone than with a sword or an axe. He was very sad when it was named after him. The guillotine chopped off tens of thousands of heads. Executions were big public events. People brought picnics and

bought programmes with the names of those
about to be killed. The guillotine chopped
off the heads of Louis XVI and Marie
Antoinette at the end of the French
Revolution. It was used for the last time
in 1977 . . .

Et cetera. Dylan's article came next.

Poltergeists: Fact or Fiction?
By Dylan Brinkerhoff

Poltergeist means 'noisy ghost' in German.
Poltergeists are different from regular
ghosts because they can move things and
even throw things. Some people think they
mean harm, and maybe some of them do, but
our poltergeist does not. That is right:
we have a poltergeist. His name is Bernard.
He is sometimes annoying, but I think he
likes being a part of our family. I think
he protects us in his own way . . .

Et cetera. Dylan and I had had to look a lot of words up
and keep the grammar simple because we didn't have a big
French vocabulary yet. My simple crossword rounded out
the second page.

Winnie's article was last. Because it was so long, Charlie
had made it single space to fit.

**Everything You Need to Know About Asbestos
and Mesothelioma
By Winnie Wu**

Mesothelioma is a cancerous tumour that starts in the cells of the *mesothelium.* What is the mesothelium? you ask. Well, it is a membrane that protects a lot of your internal organs. The one that protects our lungs is called the *pleura.* Actually, there are *two* layers, and the inner layer is called the *visceral pleura* and the outer layer is called the *parietal pleura.* Anyway, they are made up of cells. Those cells are called *mesothelial* cells. And sometimes they act up! They change and sometimes turn into cancerous cells. Why does this happen? Well, guess what: the culprit is often ASBESTOS. Asbestos fibres are very fine. And when someone breathes them in, they can get in — you guessed it — the *mesothelium.* The link between asbestos and mesothelioma has been known for years and lots of people die from it, and even though it is now illegal in Canada we still export it to other countries, which, in this reporter's opinion, is sick and wrong. But also — *newsflash* — it is still in the walls of many old buildings and — *newsflash* — that includes our very own school . . .

Winnie's article went on, and on, from there, with big words that no one but she and Monsieur Thibault could understand.

When the bell rang for lunch, a bunch of kids came up to Dylan and me to tell us they'd enjoyed our articles and had been able to follow them. One girl, Sophie, fell into a deep conversation with Dylan about the paranormal. 'Sometimes my grandma sits on my bed in the middle of the night,' I heard her say, 'and she's been dead for five years!'

No one said a word to Winnie, except for Donald. 'Your article was amazing,' he said as he walked past her desk. 'Amazingly stupid!' He and his friend Vlad cracked up.

Winnie's shoulders drooped. She scurried out of the room. Dylan and Sophie had moved on to the subject of Ouija boards, so I told him I'd see him in the cafeteria.

Winnie was sitting at a table by herself, eating an egg and bean sprout sandwich. I felt a twinge of pity, so I sat down across from her. 'I thought your article was very informative,' I said. To my utter horror, her eyes filled with tears. 'Whoa. Don't cry—'

'Last year I was diagnosed with dyscalculia.'

'That – that's awful. Is it terminal?'

She gave me a sharp look. 'What? No, dummy. It's, like, maths dyslexia. I flunked out of the Kumon maths programme! And the year before that I was asked not to sign up again for ballet lessons because I was too clumsy.' She blew her nose into a Kleenex. 'You think I'm this totally perfect person—'

'No. No, I don't. Not even close—'

'But I'm not. There are so many things I'm lousy at. And I just – I thought, journalism was my thing, you know. I thought this was the thing I was actually good at. Aside from languages, I guess.'

'Winnie, come on. It's just one article.'

'One article on a very important subject. Which nobody read.' She sighed. 'No one wants to think any more. No one wants to read anything that matters.'

'Maybe you needed to hook them more. You know, like, if the headline had been, "Is Your School Killing You?" And next time, maybe simplify. You dumped a whole bunch of big words on the reader. Even in English it would have been hard to follow.'

She'd stopped crying. 'In other words, you want me to pander to the lowest common denominator.' Her voice was icy.

'The lowest— What?'

She stood up and slapped her hands down on the table. 'I refuse to be a part of the dumbing down of North America!' Then she grabbed her gross sandwich and flounced away in her plaid skirt, and I didn't feel sorry for her any more.

• • •

After school I didn't go to Dylan's place for once. Instead I walked all the way to Bean There, Donut That with a copy of the paper under my arm. Bells jingled over the door as I walked in. The walls were painted bright yellow, making it feel warm and inviting. Astrid gave me a wave; she was behind the counter, making a fancy coffee for a customer. I put the paper down beside the machine. 'Is this what I think it is?' she asked.

I nodded. She stopped what she was doing and started reading.

After a moment, the customer cleared his throat. Astrid waved the paper in his direction. 'My kid's a published journalist!' Then she abandoned the coffee machine altogether and came around the counter to give me a hug. 'I'm so proud of you, Felix. It's excellent.'

The customer cleared his throat again, louder this time.

Astrid rolled her eyes. 'Some people should learn how to meditate,' she said, loud enough for him to hear. She finished making his coffee. Once he'd left, muttering under his breath, it was just the two of us. 'I'm going to make you a hot chocolate,' she said. 'With extra whipped cream. Because I have good news, too.'

My heart did a little flip in my chest. 'Is it about the place we saw?' On Sunday we had seen an apartment for rent, one that we both really liked. It was a garden suite, which was a fancy way of saying *basement*, but it was clean and had lots of windows, and it was close to the school.

'Yep. Landlord called, says it's ours if we want it. He just has to call my boss, get a reference. In a week I'll be able to show him my pay stub.'

Since we were celebrating, Astrid let me eat Chef Boyardee pasta for dinner when we got back to the van. We had day-old oat fudge bars from the coffee shop for dessert. Horatio loved the oats, so I fed him quite a bit. We were both giddy with the thought of having our own place again, and as we lay in our beds in the dark we talked about what we looked forward to most. 'Having a bathtub,' said Astrid.

'Having a toilet,' I said.

And also: no more lies, I thought. I didn't like lying to Dylan, or to Winnie. Soon I could have a friend over any time I wanted.

After I turned out my headlamp I only made it halfway through listing all the Nobel Peace Prize winners in my head before I fell into a deep, uninterrupted sleep.

I went to Dylan's house after school the next day, and by the time I got back to the van it was close to six o'clock. Astrid usually didn't get home until at least six-thirty, so I let myself in with my key.

She was curled up on the back seat, her sleeping bag wrapped around her.

'Astrid?'

She didn't answer.

'I thought you were working till six.'

'I was supposed to,' she said, her voice muffled through the sleeping bag.

Oh no. My P.O.O. told me something was very wrong. 'What happened?'

'My boss read all these lousy reviews about a "new barista with a bad attitude" online. I told him it wasn't my job to be nice to jerks. He said it was. Then he fired me.'

My skin felt clammy all of a sudden. 'What about the apartment?'

'The landlord called the shop for a reference five minutes after I got fired.'

'Oh.'

'I'm sorry, Felix. I really am.'

I crawled into the van and closed the door against the rain. I sat beside my mom and rubbed her back. Then I took Horatio out of his cage and held him close. His whiskers tickled my face.

I glanced up and saw Mel on the dashboard. I could have sworn he was staring right at me.

We would not be moving out of the Westfalia. Not yet.

OCTOBER

Before I continue I should probably explain the origins of my name. On my birth certificate I am Felix Fredrik Knutsson. Fredrik was my *morfar*'s name. He died before I was born. Mormor's stories about him made him sound like a saint. But Astrid says Mormor was engaged in 'revisionist history'.

'Then why did you name me after him?'

'I didn't. I named you after Eugène Fredrik Jansson, my favourite Swedish painter. Your mormor just assumed I'd named you after my father, and I let her believe it, because it kept her more or less off my back when I gave you the first name Felix.'

My mom named me after her older brother. The name is derived from Latin and means 'lucky or successful one'. Original Felix was neither.

Astrid has told me a lot about him. They were super close. He was two years older than her. She adored him, and the feeling was mutual. Felix was handsome and funny and charming, and he watched out for my mom from an early age.

Because Fredrik was a mean dad. He was very religious, but not in a nice, 'love thy neighbour' way. He was religious in more of 'an eye for an eye' way. Whenever Original Felix or Astrid stepped out of line, they would get the belt. Felix couldn't stand to see Astrid get hit, so he took the blame for everything. And he got the belt a lot.

When he was sixteen, Original Felix came out to his parents. Astrid thinks Mormor wanted to understand, because she loved Felix. But their father thought homosexuality was a sin, and he kicked Felix out of the house.

Original Felix was a smart, resourceful guy, according to my mom. But he was only sixteen. He had to make money to pay the rent on a room in a decrepit building near Main and Hastings in Vancouver. He got a part-time job at a Burger King, but it only paid minimum wage. So he did other things to earn more money, things that made him feel bad about himself and sometimes put him in danger.

He started to use drugs. Astrid would visit him every chance she got. She could see he was sinking, and she tried to get him help. But I guess there are a lot of people who need help in Vancouver, and not enough people to help them.

She was the one who found him. She hadn't heard from him for a few days, so she went to his place. He didn't answer her knocks. She got a neighbour to help her force the door. The coroner said he'd died of an accidental overdose.

Astrid says their father wept at the funeral, and it made her want to rip his eyeballs out with her bare hands.

Based on my P.O.O., I have developed a theory, and the theory is that I am not sure my mom ever completely recovered from Original Felix's death. Of course, I've only known my mom A.O.F. (After Original Felix). But it's the way she talks about him, the way she gets this look on her face. I think it destroyed a little part of her. I think it's why she has a prescription for antidepressants.

She likes to say that the day I was born was the happiest day of her life. And she named me after her brother, to keep his memory alive. I think that's why she likes me to call her Astrid instead of 'Mom', because that's what Original Felix called her.

I know some people find it weird. I remember other parents in the playground thought I was precocious, calling her Astrid. But when they found out she wanted it that way, they looked at her like *she* was precocious.

I'm just trying to give some context before I mention Astrid's Slumps. That's her word for them. *Slumps.* She's had them off and on over the years, but they usually don't last very long – a few days at most. During a Slump she stays in bed and I take charge. Mormor took charge when she was alive, but after that it was left to me.

The first time I took charge I was eight years old. I don't know what caused that particular Slump; perhaps it was because it was around the anniversary of Original Felix's death. Astrid just didn't get up one morning. So I got myself to school and I got myself home and I made us each a peanut butter and jam sandwich for dinner. I even went to bed on time, but I didn't brush my teeth.

On the third day of that Slump, my teacher asked if everything was OK at home. I said yes. She said, 'You've worn the same clothes to school all week.' The next day I changed my clothes. But one of the other mothers called my mom to say she'd seen me walking home alone again, and she gave her heck. Astrid grumbled about 'meddling helicopter parents', but the next day she managed to drag herself out of bed and walk me to and from school. 'The last thing we need is some busybody calling the MCFD.'

I think that was the first time I'd ever heard of the MCFD.

I won't lie, I was scared the first few times Astrid had a Slump and I had to take over. But I got good at it. I knew I had to ride it out for a few days, a week tops. Astrid would always assure me that she was OK, she just needed to get through it, and she always did.

She always does.

OK?

She always does.

After Astrid told me she'd been fired, I was angry. Angry at her boss. Angry at the landlord for his bad timing. But mostly, I was angry with Astrid. 'All you needed to do was keep your mouth shut and do your job!' I wanted to shout at her.

But I didn't.

It's hard to yell at a lump under the covers.

I barely slept that night. I tried to make lists, but I couldn't focus. My mind drifted to unusual places. I couldn't shake the thought that maybe we'd angered our *tomte*. I remembered everything Mormor had told me about *tomtar*. They were supposed to do their best to protect their family from harm, but they were also easily insulted. What if I hadn't paid enough attention to Mel? What if Astrid's comments about finding him creepy had made him angry? What if he was sick of living on a dashboard, in a van?

I know I fell asleep eventually, because I had a wonderful dream. I was back in Mormor's house. Mormor and I were sitting on the couch, watching *Who, What, Where, When* and eating balls of *pepparkakor* dough. I leaned into her and closed my eyes. A car alarm started blaring outside.

The car alarm kept blaring, finally pulling me out of the dream. I picked up my phone, still groggy with sleep.

It was almost nine o'clock.

I sat up so fast, I hit my head on the roof. 'How come you didn't set the alarm?' I shouted, feeling angry all over again.

I peered down from my bed. Astrid was still a lump under her sleeping bag.

'Come on, Astrid,' I said, the anger draining from my voice. 'I need you to get up. I need room to get ready.'

'Rrrmph,' she said.

I climbed down from my bed and inched the sleeping bag back from her face. 'Seriously. I'm already late.'

'Sorry, Felix. I just feel so tired.' When she's in a Slump her expression becomes lifeless, like she's had freezing at the dentist. And her voice becomes monotone, like she's been drugged.

My clean clothes were in a cubby that I could only reach once her bed was put away, so I just grabbed the jeans and striped T-shirt I'd worn the day before. I wriggled out of my pyjamas in the front seat, after making sure no one was walking by, and slipped on my clothes. Then I fed Horatio and kissed his head and hopped out of the van. 'Please try to get up today,' I said to my mom as I closed the door.

I ran the entire ten blocks to school.

• • •

'Felix, nice of you to join us,' said Monsieur Thibault in French as I walked into class half an hour late. I was sticky with sleep sweat and running sweat.

'Je m'excuse.' I slipped into my seat beside Dylan.

After a few minutes, Donald, who sat in front of me, turned around, holding his nose. 'Pee-yew, dude! You reek!' he whispered.

I felt the blood rush to my face. I glanced at Dylan, who shrugged helplessly. He slipped me a note.

He is a dingus. But he is not wrong.

Also, your T-shirt is on inside out.

I raised my hand and asked to be excused. 'You just got here,' said Monsieur Thibault. But he let me go. I went to my locker and got out my toiletry kit.

Someone was in the handicapped toilet, so I went to the regular one. Lucky for me, it was empty. I peeled off my T-shirt and gave my pits a good scrub in the sink. Then I shoved a wet paper towel down my pants to give a wipe there, too.

The door opened and a younger boy entered. He stood rooted to the spot, staring.

I decided to own the moment. I just stared right back at him, the wet paper towel still jammed down my pants. He backed out of the washroom.

I dried off, then doused my pits with deodorant and rubbed some on the inside of my T-shirt for good measure before pulling it back on, right-side out. Then I headed back to class.

A few minutes later, Dylan slipped me another note. *All good.* ☺

At lunchtime Dylan and I found a table near the back of the cafeteria. He pulled a triple-decker sandwich out of his lunch bag and started eating.

My stomach gurgled. I hadn't eaten breakfast. I hadn't brought anything for lunch. And I had no money.

Winnie approached our table and joined us without asking if it was OK. She was wiping off her black beret, which was covered in dust.

'What happened?' I asked.

'Donald used it as a Frisbee again.' She placed a cloth lunch bag on the table and started laying out her food: two egg sandwiches on her homemade bread, an apple, a banana, a yogurt, some cheese cubes, and a rather big round pastry. 'Felix, you seem discombobulated today,' she said as she started in on the first sandwich. '*Discombobulated* means—'

'I know what it means, thanks.' My stomach issued a shockingly loud growl.

'Where's your lunch?'

'I forgot it.'

She pushed one of her sandwiches towards me. 'Eat this. It's spelt bread.'

'Um. Thanks.' Beggars couldn't be choosers. I took a tentative bite. I chewed. And chewed. Dylan gave me a sympathetic look and passed me a Babybel cheese, which I devoured.

When I'd managed to get her sandwich down, Winnie cut her pastry into pieces with a cafeteria knife and handed both me and Dylan a slice. 'Try a piece of moon cake, too. My parents buy them all the time during the Moon Festival. Not super healthy, but so good. Salty egg yolks in red bean paste.'

'Yum,' said Dylan with his mouth full.

I nodded agreement; it was so good. 'Thank you.'

'I've been thinking about what to write for the next issue of the paper,' Winnie said. Her perfect red lips were speckled with egg, and I had the unbidden thought that she looked adorable. *But I don't even like her!* my inner voice said.

'I can still cover a hard-hitting topic, but I've decided that I need to hook the reader more. Simplify, too, without dumbing down.'

I stared at her. 'Those were my exact suggestions.'

She ignored me. 'We have a serious housing crisis in this city. Prices are through the roof. Our homeless population is already big, and continues to grow. So instead of just throwing out statistics, I was thinking –' she took another bite of her sandwich and kept talking with her mouth full – 'every day when I walk from the bus stop to school, I see the same guy sleeping in a storefront. He calls himself Bob the Bard. I'd like to interview him. Ask him what it's like to be homeless.'

I felt nauseous all of a sudden, and it wasn't Winnie's sandwich.

It may sound nuts, but it was the first time it hit me that, technically speaking, *I* was homeless. Astrid and I had a van, but we didn't have a home. It hadn't bothered me before because I'd never thought it would last.

Now, after yesterday, I wasn't so sure.

I went straight home after school.

Or should I say, *straight van.*

Astrid was still in bed.

'Have you been lying there all day?'

'No. I've been out.'

I peeled her sleeping bag back. 'No, you haven't. You're still in your pyjamas.'

'I got out of my pyjamas. I went out. I came back. I put my pyjamas back on.'

'Liar.'

'Felix. Back off, please. I can't take it.'

I wanted to plead with her. I wanted to tell her that the longer this Slump lasted, the longer it would take for her to find another job. But I also knew that when she was in the middle of a Slump, there was no point. 'Fine. But you have to get up now. We need to fold away your bed to get to the stove. I'll cook.'

She did as she was told. I heated up two tins of stew. She only had a few mouthfuls. I ate the rest. Then she dozed on the back seat while I sat up front, doing homework. I let Horatio out of his cage and he ran up one of my arms and down the other.

When I was done with my homework I dug out a packet of instant oatmeal. I put the kettle on to boil. I poured the water over the oats and stirred.

Before I'd left the school cafeteria, I'd taken a pat of butter from the condiments counter. Now I took it out of my backpack, unwrapped it, and placed it on the porridge.

Mormor had told me that you could appease an angry *tomte* by giving him a bowl of porridge with butter on top. So I put the bowl on the dashboard, in front of Mel.

'This is for you,' I whispered. 'I'm sorry if we offended you in any way.'

Hey. It was worth a try.

Astrid's Slump lasted three days.

I made sure to put out clean clothes and make lunch the night before and set my own alarm. I left plenty of time to go to school early so I could wash in the handicapped washroom.

On the fourth day, Astrid got up with me. She drove us to a community centre so we could shower for the first time in six days. 'Why is there a congealed bowl of porridge on the dash?' she asked, but I pretended I hadn't heard.

Our membership had expired long ago. So we did what we always did: we waited until the receptionist at the front desk was occupied with other people, then we strode past, Astrid waving her expired membership card in his general direction.

It had worked every time, until today.

'Excuse me, ma'am!' the receptionist called after her. 'I need to see your card.'

'Oh, sure.' Astrid walked back to the desk and handed it to him.

The receptionist studied it. 'This expired over a year ago.'

'What? Are you sure?' This time my mom's lie fooled no one.

She bought us a new membership. 'We *have* money,' she said as we headed for the changing rooms. 'Just not a lot. I don't like to spend it unless I absolutely have to.'

That night we moved the Westfalia to a quiet street near Kits Beach. We made macaroni cheese and ate it wearing our coats because it was raining, and cold air seeped into the van. I let Horatio hunker down in my coat pocket. And I finally let out a thought that had been looping over and over in my brain. 'Maybe we should tell someone.'

'About what?'

'About our situation.'

Astrid put down her plastic camping spoon. 'Who would you suggest we tell?'

'Daniel?'

She shook her head. 'Absolutely not.'

'Soleil? If she knew our situation, maybe she'd let us stay at her house for a while, just until we get back on our feet.'

'Felix. Soleil has been texting me, asking when we'll be moving our things out of her basement.'

'Yes, but that's because she doesn't know the truth—'

'And she's not going to.'

'Why?'

'Because. If she knew the truth, she'd go into help mode.'

Exactly! 'Would that be so bad?'

'Yes, it would. She'd get the Ministry of Children and Family Development involved, I guarantee it.'

Some kids grow up with scary stories about monsters, or ghosts, or bogeymen under the bed. My scary stories were about the MCFD. And unlike the ones about monsters, ghosts and bogeymen, these stories weren't make-believe.

As I already mentioned, I'd had one brief encounter with the MCFD. But that was nothing compared with Astrid's experience.

When Astrid was ten and Original Felix was twelve, their father gave Felix a particularly bad beating. My mom couldn't take it. She snuck away and called the police. Fredrik and the kids were questioned in separate rooms. Then a social worker from the MCFD arrived. Astrid and Felix were removed from the house and sent to foster homes.

Different foster homes. For two whole months they didn't see each other. They lived with strangers, in homes with other foster kids. Astrid's foster parents were kind, and the other kids weren't too bad. Original Felix wasn't so lucky.

When they were finally able to go back home, they both agreed: getting the odd beating and verbal smackdown from a mean dad was better any day than the so-called help they'd received.

I didn't want the MCFD to take me away from my mom and put me in a home with mean strangers and possibly violent kids. But still. 'Maybe, if we asked the right people, there might be some sort of social housing we could get into—'

'You and I are *not* living in social housing.' That was her strange snobbery at work. Somehow we were too good to live in social housing, but living in a van was OK.

I fed Horatio another piece of lettuce.

Astrid put an arm around me. 'I'll find another job, Böna. It'll be fine. I promise.'

I wanted to believe her. I really did.

But I was pretty sure she'd just told a Give Peace a Chance.

'Want to sleep over on Friday?' Dylan asked me mid-week. His hair was smooshed to his skull on one side and puffed out on the other in a particularly spectacular case of bed-head.

'Sure!' I said, a little too enthusiastically. The thought of a real bed, indoor plumbing, heating and, most of all, Dylan's fridge, made me feel positively giddy.

On Friday morning I packed an overnight bag. 'Are you going to be OK while I'm gone?' I asked my mom.

She smiled. 'Yes, Lilla Gubben. I've been wanting to do my yearly reread of *Middlemarch,* so I might just do that.'

'Promise me you'll get out.'

'I will. I'm going to go to the library. Polish up my résumé.' I knew *polish* was probably code for 'embellish'. But if it meant she was looking for work, I didn't care.

'I have a hankering for a game of Monopoly,' Dylan said at the end of the day. 'We can have an epic session. Plus my mom went to Costco yesterday, so we have epic snacks.' I thought I might burst from too much happiness.

We were no more than ten seconds from the front doors of the school – so close, and yet so far – when Winnie approached. She was wearing her green beret. 'I was wondering if I could ask you guys a favour.'

Uh-oh.

'I'm going to try to interview Bob the Bard. And I'm embarrassed to admit to my own biases and fears, but I'm a little nervous. I mean, he might not be happy if I try to talk to him, he might be unstable – I just don't know. Would you mind coming with me?'

'Does it have to be today?' I asked.

'If I don't do it today, I won't get the article done on time.'

Dylan and looked at each other and sighed.

Bob the Bard is a Kitsilano institution. He was on the same corner when Astrid and I had our apartment, and he was there now as we approached. He had a little jar in front of him that had some coins in it, and a sign that read POEMS FOR SALE. TWO BUCKS.

'Hello,' Winnie said, a slight quaver in her voice.

'Afternoon. Want a poem?'

'Um. No—' Winnie began, but I gave her a nudge. 'I mean, sure.' Winnie handed him two dollars. Bob flipped through a notebook, which was covered in spindly hand-writing. He tore out a page and read it aloud. '*A child laughs, clutching a red balloon. A girlfriend laughs at something her boyfriend has said. An old man laughs at a voice in his head.*

The crow laughs at them all from its perch on the tree, above.'
He held out the poem. His hands were dirty, his skin
cracked. Winnie's mouth made a little O of horror.

I reached out and grabbed the poem. 'Thanks. That was
very nice,' I said.

'I call it "Laughter,"' said Bob the Bard.

'Deep,' said Dylan.

Winnie cleared her throat. 'I was also wondering if
I could interview you for our school paper. About, um –'
she coughed, embarrassed – 'homelessness.'

Bob the Bard squinted at her. He held out his hand.
Winnie looked at it, confused. 'He wants more money,'
I whispered.

Winnie handed him another two-dollar coin. Bob the
Bard gave her a withering look. 'Interviews cost more than
poems.'

Winnie dug into her satchel and handed him a ten-dollar
bill. 'If I could have five back—'

Bob pocketed the ten. 'Ask away.'

Winnie pressed Record on her phone. 'How long have
you been homeless?'

'Almost twenty years. I'm fifty-one now.'

Dylan and I glanced at each other; Bob looked much,
much older.

'What did you do before you lived on the street?'

'I was a regular guy. University degree. Job in middle
management. Wife, kids.'

'What happened?'

'Company downsized. I lost my job. We were in a recession. Couldn't find work. Got depressed. Started drinking. Wife left me. Kids and I grew apart. I was too educated to get a McJob, and when I did manage to land one, it never lasted very long because I was like a fossil, the young kids were so much better at handling all the computerised systems than I was.' As he kept talking, I felt goose bumps on my arms, even though I was wearing a jacket. 'Lost my apartment. Lost my friends . . . started sleeping in shelters. But shelters are awful. Full of crazies and bedbugs and thieves. I feel safer out here than I do in one of those places.' He gazed up at Winnie. 'You think it'll never happen to you. Well, guess what. It can happen to anyone.'

I knew he was telling the truth. Because Astrid and I were already halfway there.

Winnie gave Bob the Bard a sandwich that she'd made especially for him before we said goodbye. As we walked away, I saw him take a bite, spit it out, and toss the sandwich in the garbage. Clearly some beggars *could* be choosers.

'So. Where to now?' asked Winnie.

'Um, we're going to Dylan's house—' I started.

'Goody.' She skipped ahead of us. Dylan pretended to wrap a noose around his neck and hang himself. I pretended to fall on a sword.

When we got to the Brinkerhoffs', Dylan and I got

Cheezies and taquitos to bring into the living room while Winnie lectured us on the health hazards of eating processed food. We responded by opening cans of root beer, taking big swigs and belching loudly. 'You're both disgusting,' she said. We belched again.

We played Monopoly. Not surprisingly, Winnie was super competitive, and a sore winner; she lorded it over us long after we'd put the game away.

To shut her up, Dylan put on the TV. *Who, What, Where, When* was on, so we shouted out answers at the TV screen; Winnie knew almost as many as I did.

Just before a commercial break the announcer said, 'We're launching our first-ever week-long *Who, What, Where, When – Junior Edition*! Want to be a contestant? Take our online questionnaire to see if you're eligible.'

Dylan muted the TV and looked at us. 'Let's do it.'

Winnie raised an eyebrow. 'No offence, but I'll crush you both.'

'You'll crush me,' said Dylan. 'But I bet you won't crush Felix.'

Winnie had her laptop with her and Dylan had his. I used the desktop computer in the kitchen. After we'd filled in some personal information, we were directed to the quiz. It was based on two criteria; the time it took to complete it, and how many questions we got right. There were fifty questions in all. Here's a small sample:

Who wrote Lord of the Flies? (William Golding)

Where would you find the Great Barrier Reef? (Australia)

What luxury liner did a German submarine sink in 1915? (the *Lusitania*)

When did America join World War II? (December 1941)

Dylan took eight minutes and forty seconds, and got twenty-six questions right.

Winnie took seven minutes and eight seconds, and got forty-one questions right.

I took six minutes and fifty seconds.

And I got forty-six questions right.

'Holy crap, Felix,' said Dylan. 'That's amazing.'

'Lucky break,' said Winnie.

'It's not luck,' Dylan said. 'I've seen him do it before. Felix is really smart.'

'Huh,' she said. 'Who knew?'

A few moments later we all got the same email:

Thank you for your interest. Due to the high volume of applicants, it will take two to three weeks to process your entry. If you are chosen for an audition, you will be informed at that time.

'Well,' Winnie announced as she shut down her laptop, 'sorry, you guys, but it's time for me to hit the road.'

'What a shame,' said Dylan.

The Brinkerhoffs came home soon after Winnie left.

• • •

'Felix!' said Mrs Brinkerhoff. 'We finally get to lay eyes on you.' She pulled me in for a hug and I noticed she still smelled like vanilla. Mr Brinkerhoff – who is like a carbon copy of his dishevelled son, only taller, rounder and without braces – shook my hand.

'Great to see you again. How's your mom?'

'Good. Really good.'

I told myself it was an Invisible Lie.

The Brinkerhoffs ordered Thai food for dinner. Alberta and her boyfriend, Henry, were there, and the six of us crowded around the kitchen table. Dylan and I told them about the online quiz, and Henry asked us to repeat a bunch of the questions. He got them all right. 'You two have a freakish ability to retain information,' Alberta said.

I ate so much I could stick out my stomach in an unsightly way. There was lots of laughing and arguing and the room was big and warm and bright.

That night I lay in Dylan's lower bunk bed while he told me a story about Bernard. 'He moved all my clothes around while I was at school. Put all my underwear into my T-shirt drawer, and I found my T-shirts under my bed! But he never does anything mean. He's a good poltergeist.' I don't remember anything after that because I fell asleep and slept for twelve hours.

We ate a late breakfast of pancakes with buckets of butter and maple syrup. The bubble finally burst when

Dylan's mom reminded him that he had a karate lesson at one.

'We can drive you home,' said Mrs Brinkerhoff. 'I'd love to say a quick hello to Astrid. It's been ages since I've seen her.'

'It's OK. She's at work today, and I have things to do on the way home anyway.' A No One Gets Hurt.

You know when you have a really awesome dream, the kind where everything is just perfect and magical? Like, you've just found a trunk full of your favourite chocolate bars under your bed? And then you wake up, and the letdown is enormous? That's how it felt as I trudged the two kilometres to Kits Beach, to our Westfalia, and to my mom.

Astrid and I had a Sunday routine. We stayed in bed until ten; then we went to the community centre to use their exercise equipment and have a hot shower. Afterwards we went for breakfast at the Cozy Café on Dunbar Street, which has a full bacon-and-egg breakfast for just $4.99. When we were done, we did our laundry, followed by grocery shopping at the No Frills.

On this particular Sunday I was loading up the cart with cans of dented soup when I saw something out of the corner of my eye. Something I wish I hadn't seen:

Astrid, slipping a package of sausages into her coat pocket.

My inner voice said, *Maybe I only think I saw that. Maybe I made a mistake. Maybe she made a mistake. Maybe she slipped it into her coat by accident. Like that time I put my homework in the fridge.*

But in the next aisle, I saw her slip a bag of almonds into her purse. 'Astrid,' I said in a voice only she could hear. 'I saw what you did.'

'Hmm?'

'You have sausages in your coat pocket and a bag of almonds in your purse.'

'Don't forget the hunk of Brie.' She actually smiled.

'That's stealing!'

'Only if you use capitalist thinking. I look at it through a different lens. I buy the things that are reasonably priced. I only pocket items that are marked up ridiculously high. Stores like this rob us blind by charging those prices. They're a part of the capitalist system. I'm just levelling the playing field.'

'But it's a No Frills!'

'Böna, it's still a business. And I plan on buying everything else in this cart. They'll still make a profit off us. Think of me as your own personal Robin Hood.' She pushed the cart around the corner and into the next aisle.

Astrid's argument made my head hurt, and I didn't know how to respond. When we approached the counter, I stood in front of the cart, blocking her path. I spoke in a whisper. 'If you get caught—'

'The only way I'll get caught is if you keep acting like there's something up. So cut it out.' She gave me one of those smiles that wasn't a smile.

We joined the line. I was sweating with fear. But Astrid was cool as a cucumber as she started placing our groceries onto the conveyor belt.

The sullen cashier had all sorts of piercings. The one in her forehead looked painful and infected.

I started to hiccup.

Suddenly I felt really angry. Astrid was putting us in a new kind of danger.

I grabbed a chocolate bar from the rack and threw it onto the conveyor belt.

Astrid gave me a warning look. 'Fine. One chocolate bar—'

I threw down two more, still hiccuping, daring her with my eyes to tell me I couldn't. She stared at me hard, then shrugged at the cashier, who must have been medicated; she had no expression whatsoever.

'Fifty-four eighty,' said the cashier.

Astrid opened her purse and rummaged for her wallet. I could see the bag of almonds, sitting on top. I started to sweat again. If I could see them, surely the cashier could. I bagged the groceries. We walked out of the store. I kept waiting for a security guard to come chasing after us and tackle us to the ground.

Nothing happened.

Astrid loaded the bags into the back of the van. 'See? All that worry for nothing.'

'If you'd been caught—'

'But I wasn't.'

'But if you were—'

'But I wasn't.' She said this in a tone that meant *Drop it right now or else.* Then she tossed me one of my chocolate bars. 'There's a free concert outside the CBC building in an hour. Want to go?'

We went. And I didn't mention the shoplifting again.

• • •

I'd like to be able to say that the food Astrid stole tasted like sawdust in my mouth. But it didn't. It tasted delicious. We had the Brie on crackers as a pre-dinner snack. And the sausages, fried up in a pan, tossed with a pot of spaghetti, were mouthwateringly good. Even Horatio ate a piece of the Brie and loved it, but we paid for it later because it gave him wicked diarrhoea, which stank up the van even after I washed his cage, and him, in one of the beach washrooms.

I'd also like to tell you that her shoplifting never happened again. But as time marched on and our bank account dwindled, Astrid did what she felt she had to do.

It really bothered me when she shoplifted from smaller stores, like Ahmadi Grocery on Broadway. We went there because their produce was well priced, so it didn't seem right when I saw Astrid slip some grapes into her purse one day, or a bag of avocados another. The owner of that store wasn't getting rich. He wasn't part of *the system*.

'Maybe we can go to a food bank,' I suggested one night.

She looked at me like I'd asked her to commit murder. 'We do *not* need to visit a food bank.' Her weird snobbery again.

I should make clear that as soon as we are able, we have every intention of paying each store what we owe them.

Well. Maybe Astrid doesn't. But I do.

I've been keeping a ledger. I have it with me.

No Frills		Ahmadi Grocery		Safeway	
bag almonds	$7.99	grapes (500g)	$2.99	muesli	$3.99
brie	$8.49	avocados (bag)	$4.99	soap	$4.99
sausages	$6.50	apples (4)	approx $2.00	aspirin	$6.99
dark chocolate w. sea salt	$5.25	bananas (4)	$2.00		
		mango	$1.50		
Häagen-Dazs ice cream	$7.50	tomatoes, cherry	$2.99		
aged cheddar	$9.32				
digestive biscuits	$2.99				
prosciutto	$6.99				
steak	$10.20				
deodorant	$4.99				

Once we come into some money – which is going to happen very, very soon – I'll go to the stores we stole from and set up a repayment plan.

I'm not sure how I'll explain it.

But that's a worry for another day.

By mid-October the weather was getting worse. Colder. A lot more rain.

One night we were huddled in the van, bickering. Even though it was only six o'clock, it was pitch-dark outside. 'I'm freezing,' I said. 'Horatio's freezing.'

'So you've said. Twenty thousand times.'

'Mel is freezing.'

'Now you're being ridiculous.'

'And I'm bored out of my mind and I'm claustrophobic and it smells like old farts in here—'

Suddenly Astrid moved into the driver's seat and turned the key in the ignition.

'Where are we going?'

She didn't answer. She just drove, up the hill and west, into the neighbourhood of Point Grey.

She turned onto a block that seemed almost deserted. A lot of the homes were brand new and appeared empty. She pointed to one that was maybe two-thirds complete. 'I've driven past this one a few times. No one's living there, I'm sure of it. And also, the garage door isn't locked.'

'How do you know that?'

She didn't answer. She just turned off the van's lights and drove down the back alley. She motioned for me to get out and open the garage door. 'Astrid—' I started.

'It's your choice, Felix. You can open the door, or we can go back to the beach.'

I opened the door.

My worry evaporated after the first couple of nights. Whatever laws we might be breaking, it was worth it. When we lowered the door, no one knew we were in there. There was electricity, so we could turn on the overhead lights and plug in our fridge and keep stuff like milk and eggs, and we could read as late as we wanted. There were power outlets to charge our ancient laptop and our phones. We ate in our camping chairs inside the garage, but outside the van. It felt positively palatial. And because there was a tap beside the house, we could even fill up some buckets after dark and heat up the water on the stove in the mornings and wash our bits.

And yes, when it was dark, we peed in the yard.

But only peed.

Except once, when it was an emergency.

The houses to the left and right and directly behind us also appeared to be empty, but still, we were cautious when we came or went. It meant a much longer walk to school for me, but I didn't mind. I felt better rested than I had in a while. Astrid looked less tired, too.

At school one morning, the girl doing the announcements said, 'Mark next Friday on your calendars – it's the first school dance of the year! Invite that special someone, or come with your friends and dance the night away! Well, until ten p.m., when the school shuts us down!'

'School dances are a joke,' Winnie declared at lunchtime. We sat across from each other in the cafeteria; Dylan was in line, buying fries. 'Archaic. I should write a scathing exposé for the November paper.' Winnie had completed her article on Bob the Bard for the October edition. It wouldn't be out until the end of the month, but she was already hunting around for her next idea.

'A scathing exposé on school dances?'

'Yes! They only disappoint. They set up unrealistic expectations. Sure, they say you don't need a date, just go with your friends! But secretly all these poor girls – and boys, but usually girls *even though it is the twenty-first century* – are waiting to be asked. Hearts get broken. Tears are shed.'

'Um. Are you talking from personal experience?'

'No,' she said. A little too quickly.

'So you're not going?'

'Of course I'm going! With you.'

I almost spit out a piece of my bologna sandwich. 'Huh?'

'Research! I have to be there to be able to write about it, don't I?'

'Couldn't you just go by yourself?'

'No, dodo. Then I'd be too conspicuous.'

'So I'll be, like, your cover?'

'Yes.'

My brain hurt. 'Um . . . OK?'

'Good. You can pick me up at my place at seven p.m. And for a corsage, I'd prefer wrist, and nothing pink.' Winnie took a huge bite of her sandwich.

What had just happened?

And also, what the heck was a *corsage*?

Dylan and I talked about it on the walk to his house after school. 'Yeah, Sophie asked me,' he said glumly.

'What did you say?'

'Yes. But, I don't know . . . a dance? Ugh. I won't be able to wear this.' He glanced down at his uniform of wrinkled T-shirt and frayed jeans.

I felt a little ball of anxiety in my stomach. 'You think we have to dress up?' I only had one set of nice clothes. And it was in Soleil's basement.

'Probably.' He let out a heavy sigh. 'I'd rather have bamboo shoots stuck under my fingernails.'

I thought for a moment. 'I'd rather lie in a tub full of cockroaches.'

'I'd rather eat maggots for lunch.'

'I'd rather slide naked down a razor blade into a pool of iodine.'

That one cracked us up so hard, we had to stop to catch our breath.

When I got back to the garage that evening, Astrid was making sloppy joes for dinner and singing along to an old Monkees song on the radio. Even though it was cold outside, it was warm and toasty in our makeshift home. The space heater Abelard had left behind was running full blast. She grabbed my hand and twirled me around, then started kissing the top of my head.

'Aargh, stop!' I said.

She let go.

'You're in a good mood.'

'I had a couple of good interviews today,' she said.

'That's great.'

'Fingers crossed.'

I started singing, too. '*Now I'm a believer!*' I fed Horatio and got out our plates. When we sat down to eat, I shared my news. 'I've sort of been invited to a dance.'

'Really? Boy? Girl?' Astrid believes that a parent should never assume a child's sexuality.

'Girl. Winnie Wu.'

'Winnie. What a pretty name. Do you like her?'

I opened my mouth to say no – but I stopped.

Because it wasn't true.

The truth was, Winnie Wu had grown on me.

'Sort of,' I admitted. 'But she's very strong-willed and bossy and opinionated.'

Astrid smiled. 'Then I like her already. And if she likes you, she has excellent taste.' She ruffled my hair.

'But the thing is, she wants me to buy her a thing called a corsage. And I need to dress up, at least a little. And my smart trousers and shirt are at Soleil's.'

Astrid nibbled on a cookie. 'No worries. I've got it figured out.'

I wished I could say that made me feel better.

'OK, I think we're good to go in,' Astrid said. We were standing across the street from Soleil's house, sporting dark sunglasses and hats, which I thought made us look more conspicuous. We'd taken the bus instead of driving the van, because, as Astrid pointed out, Soleil knew exactly what our van looked like, down to its THE ROAD TO ENLIGHT-ENMENT HAS NO SPEED LIMIT bumper sticker (Abelard's addition, not ours).

Soleil and her husband had just driven away with the twins in their Volvo station wagon. The kids were in football uniforms.

My hiccups started as we made our way towards the back alley. 'I still don't understand why we didn't just call her—'

'For the thousandth time, Felix, she'd ask too many

questions. And remember, it's not breaking in. We're simply getting a few things that belong to us.'

'It's breaking in if we're doing it behind her – *hic!* – back,' I said. 'She doesn't know we have a key. She doesn't know we know – *hic!* – her alarm code.'

'Meaning she'll also never know we were here. It will be like it never happened. You know that expression, "If a tree falls in the forest and no one is around to hear it, does it make a sound?"'

'Yeah, but if someone *is* around, like if Soleil comes home and catches us, *she'll* make a sound,' I said as we entered their yard through the back gate.

Astrid turned to me. 'Do you want your dress clothes or not? I'm trying to help you here.' She inserted her key in the lock and opened the door. The alarm system gave off its high-pitched noise. Astrid punched in some numbers.

The noise continued.

She tried again.

It still didn't work.

'She's changed the code.' We stood frozen. My whole body felt numb, and I worried I might collapse in a heap. 'The alarm's going to start wailing in about thirty more seconds,' Astrid continued. 'Walk out through the back gate. Don't run. Walk. Meet me at the bus stop.'

'But, Mom—'

'Go.'

So I did what she said. I walked slowly, even though every bone in my body told me to run as fast as I could.

As I left the yard, the alarm started to wail. It was so loud, I could still hear it when I was two blocks away.

I waited at the bus stop for what felt like for ever but was probably five minutes. Then I saw Astrid walking towards me, calm and confident and wheeling one of our large suitcases. 'I grabbed what I could. We won't be able to go back there for a while.'

The bus came a minute later. I collapsed in a seat near the back, hiccuping over and over.

Astrid reached into her jacket pocket and pulled out a wad of twenty-dollar bills. She handed me two of them. 'Buy Winnie a wrist corsage. Maybe a yellow rose. She'll like that. And use what's left over for whatever you like.'

My mind flashed to the purse I'd seen lying just inside Soleil's back door.

I pocketed the money without a word.

The suit didn't fit.

I stood in the middle of the garage, tugging at the navy sleeves as if that would make them grow longer. I'd been noticing lately that my trousers and sweaters all seemed short and tight, like they'd shrunk in the wash.

Astrid stated the obvious. 'You've grown.'

'The dance is in two days.'

'Don't worry, Lilla Gubben. We'll just have to take you shopping.'

'But we don't have much money.'

'So? We've always been awesome thrifters. And there are some great second-hand stores near here.'

The next day after school we hit two different shops, one run by the Salvation Army and the other by the SPCA. I did really well. I got a new pair of jeans, three T-shirts and a sweater, and, for the dance, a button-up shirt, suit trousers and a suit jacket. Astrid peeled off no more than two of those twenty-dollar bills to pay for it all.

My favourite find was a red polo shirt that looked almost brand new. It had a small grease stain on the bottom front, but you could hardly see it. 'The colour looks great with your skin tone and hair,' Astrid said.

On Friday morning, Dylan told me his dad had offered to drive the four of us. 'We can come get you,' Dylan said. 'I still haven't seen where you live.'

'It's OK. I'll just come to your house. Really. My place is out of your way.'

I stopped at the florist after school to pick up Winnie's wrist corsage. When I got back to the garage, Astrid was already there, ironing my shirt and trousers on a piece of cardboard propped on top of a recycling bin. 'Since when do we own an iron?'

'Since today. I can't have my boy looking anything less than super-duper for his first dance.'

I made a face. 'Super-duper?'

When she was done ironing, I climbed into the van and changed. The trousers were a little more threadbare than I remembered and the sleeves of the jacket were a bit frayed and there was a hole in one of the pockets, but other than that, it looked great. When I stepped out, Astrid whistled. 'You look amazing.' She combed out my hair, giving it maximum volume. 'Let me see the wrist corsage.' I showed her the yellow rose in its plastic container. 'It's perfect. She'll love it.'

Astrid fed me a quick dinner, then walked with me to the Brinkerhoffs'. It was a crisp, cool night. The stars were bright. When we arrived I asked, 'Do you want to come in and say hi?'

She shook her head. 'I think I won't.' I noticed there were tears in her eyes. 'Your first dance. I love you, Felix.'

'I love you, Astrid.'

She kissed my forehead and walked away.

Alberta opened the door. 'Oh my God, you look way too cute,' she said, mussing my hair.

Dylan catapulted down the stairs. His dress shirt was wrinkled, and it was only half-tucked into his grey trousers but he still looked neater and tidier than I'd ever seen him. 'Dad, let's go!'

While we waited for Mr Brinkerhoff we endured Alberta's teasing. 'Do you have condoms?'

'Shut up,' said Dylan.

'We don't want any teen pregnancies.'

'Doofus! We're barely thirteen!'

'They say kids are getting started younger and younger these days.'

Thankfully Mr Brinkerhoff appeared, and we were off.

We picked Sophie up first. She wore pleather leggings and a hot-pink top. Mr Brinkerhoff introduced himself; Dylan just grunted. 'So, Sophie,' said Mr Brinkerhoff, trying to fill the silence, 'how's seventh grade treating you?'

'Fine.'

No one said another word on the rest of the drive to Winnie's.

I hopped out when we arrived at her building. Winnie was waiting in the lobby with her mom. She wore a shimmery silver sleeveless dress that stopped just above her knees and silver ballet flats. A white shawl was draped around her shoulders.

She looked, just . . . *wow*.

'You must be Felix,' her mom said. 'I'm Eleanor, Winnie's mom.'

'Pleased to meet you, Eleanor.' We shook hands. 'You deliver babies.'

'Yes, I do.'

Winnie cleared her throat. 'Why, thank you, Felix, you look nice, too.'

'Huh?'

Eleanor smiled. 'I think my rather rude daughter is fishing for a compliment.'

Oh. 'You look nice,' I said. Winnie's expression darkened. 'Very nice?'

'Please have her home by eleven,' Eleanor said.

'I will.' We turned to leave the building. Winnie cleared her throat. Once. Twice. 'You coming down with something?'

'Take my arm.'

Eleanor gave me an encouraging smile. I took Winnie's arm. *'Duì nǐ de péngyǒu hǎo yī diǎn,'* she called after us.

'She told me to be nice to you in Mandarin,' Winnie explained. 'Since when am I not nice?'

Halfway to the car I remembered the box in my hand. 'Oh yeah. Here's your corsage thingy.' I handed it to her and kept walking.

Winnie stopped. 'Felix.'

'What?'

'Take it out of the box and put it on my wrist.'

'Why can't you do it?'

'Because you're *supposed* to do it.'

'But this isn't even *supposed* to be a real date!' She glared at me. My P.O.O. told me this was going very badly, but I had no idea why. 'Fine!' I slipped the corsage onto her wrist. 'You happy now?'

'No!'

The drive to the school was short but deadly. Mr Brinkerhoff tried to crack jokes. 'Where do Canadians keep their armies?' No one answered. 'Up their sleevies!' We filed silently out of the car. 'For God's sake, try to have fun!' he shouted after us.

The gym had been decorated with streamers and balloons. The lights were dim. No one was dancing yet. Kids stood on the perimeter of the dance floor, eating snacks or goofing around.

I brought Winnie a glass of punch. She stood with her arms across her chest, scowling. 'Winnie. Forgive me if I'm confused. You told me I was your cover. That this was research for the school paper. Then you want me to behave all . . . datelike.'

'For a supposedly smart guy, you're really stupid.'

'What?'

'Did it honestly never occur to you that I like you?'

No. It had not. I suddenly felt very warm inside, in a not-unpleasant way.

'See, this is what I hate about school dances,' she continued. 'They get hopes up, and then those hopes are crushed, and you feel embarrassed and humiliated.'

A slow song came on.

'Anyway, do whatever you want. It's not your fault, it's mine.'

'Winnie—'

'I'm the idiot here, not you. Me.'

'Winnie—'

'Story of my life, really, you probably haven't noticed but I'm not the greatest reader of social cues—'

'*Winnie.*' She shut up. I held out my hand. She looked at it, puzzled, then her eyes lit up. I walked her to the middle of the dance floor. We were the first couple out there. I put my arms around her waist. I'd never slow-danced in my life, so I just shuffled around in a little circle.

After a while, more kids joined us. Winnie rested her head on my shoulder, which felt nice.

We only left the dance floor twice, once for snacks and once to pee.

Winnie never wrote her scathing exposé on school dances.

• • •

Mr Brinkerhoff picked us up just after ten. We dropped Winnie off first, then Sophie. Once Sophie was out of the car, Dylan exhaled loudly from the front seat. 'Thank God that's over. That was awful! I'm so sweaty!' It wasn't from dancing; he and Sophie had barely hit the dance floor.

'I thought you liked her,' Mr Brinkerhoff said.

'I thought I did, too. But then she said that she thinks poltergeists are restless spirits who want to cause pain and suffering, and I was like, "That is so not Bernard!" Bernard's a practical joker, but he looks out for us, too! And she wasn't buying it. And I was like, "How do you know? *I'm* the one with the poltergeist!"'

I caught Mr Brinkerhoff's eye in the rearview mirror, and he winked. 'Felix, where do you live?' he asked.

'It's out of your way. Just drop me at the bus stop.'

'Absolutely not. We're driving you home.'

'But—'

'No buts. What's the address?'

I drew a blank. How could I give them an address when I didn't *have* an address?

I remembered I'd told Dylan I lived on the edge of the catchment area on the first day of school. So I blurted out the one address I knew that fit that description.

Soleil's.

As we drove further and further away from the van, Mr Brinkerhoff told us stories about school dances he'd been to when he was young. I couldn't concentrate. Halfway there, I started to hiccup. As we pulled up outside Soleil's house, Dylan's dad wrapped up his latest tale. 'Never a good idea to vomit on your date's new shoes!'

He stopped the car. Dylan gave a low whistle. 'Wow. Nice digs, Felix!'

'We're just – *hic!* – renting the basement.'

Mr Brinkerhoff turned off the ignition. He started to get out of the car. 'I'll walk you to the door. Say a quick hi to your mom.'

'You can't!' I said, louder than I meant to. 'I mean – she's out. On a date. But I'll tell her – *hic!* – you said hi.'

He looked at me for a few seconds longer than was comfortable. 'OK. Well. We'll just wait here till you get inside.'

'Great. Thanks for the ride.' I got out of the car, my suit jacket flung over my arm. I walked across the street. There were still a couple of lights on in Soleil's house, including, thank goodness, one in the basement.

I walked down the path at the side of the house. I opened the gate. A floodlight went on, with me directly in the beam. *Please, please, don't let anyone look outside.*

I waved once more to Dylan and his dad. As gently as I could, I closed the gate. I tiptoed through Soleil's yard to the back gate, the one that led into the alley. A dog started barking inside the house.

Soleil and her family had got a dog. Maybe they'd gotten a dog because they were afraid. Maybe they were afraid because someone had recently broken into their house.

I fled through the back gate. The arm of my brand-new used dress shirt got caught on something, and I heard a ripping sound. More lights went on in the house, and I heard the back door open. 'Who's out there?' Soleil's husband, Arpad.

I ran down the alley. When I was a few blocks away, I pulled out my phone and texted Dylan: *Safe inside!*

The beautiful, clear night had turned frosty and cold. I pulled the suit jacket on, but I shivered as I waited for the bus, which was late. When it finally arrived I sat by one of the heaters, trying to warm up. I inspected the tear in my shirt. It was about eight centimetres long. I wanted to cry.

But I didn't.

After all, it had been a mostly wonderful night.

The rest of the weekend was long and dull. Dylan had a karate tournament, and Winnie had to go to her cousin's wedding. 'I love seeing my *gōng gōng* and *pōpō,* but these things go on for ever. We have to sit through a ten-course banquet. Ten courses!' she'd complained the night before. I wanted to say 'Ten courses! Can I come?'

Astrid and I filled our time doing our laundry and our shopping. On Sunday afternoon we went to the library to get out some books and to use their free Wi-Fi.

I had an email.

Congratulations, Felix Knutsson! You've been selected to audition for a spot on *Who, What, Where, When – Junior Edition.* Auditions will be held on Tuesday, October 30, at the Holiday Inn, downtown Vancouver. Please arrive by nine a.m. at the latest for check-in. And good luck!

    Sincerely,

    Nazneen Iravani

    Producer

I showed Astrid. We whooped so loudly that the librarian had to shush us three times.

I told Dylan on Monday morning when we arrived at school. 'That is amazing, Felix!' he said. 'I got an email, too. A *thanks, but no thanks*.'

We ran into Winnie on the front steps. She'd bought herself a brand-new beret in canary yellow, and matching canary-yellow socks. 'You look . . . bright,' I said.

'Like Tweety Bird,' added Dylan.

Any fears I'd had that it would be weird between us after the dance disappeared when she launched right in. 'I heard from *Who, What, Where, When*. I got an audition.' She was trying really hard not to look smug.

'That's awesome,' I said. 'Congratulations.'

'Wow,' said Dylan. 'I can't believe I know *two* people who got an audition!'

Winnie blinked. 'Oh. Felix got an audition, too?'

'Yep,' I replied.

It took her a moment before she said, 'Well. Congratulations to you, too.'

She did not sound entirely sincere.

We had only a week to prepare, and we made the most of it. Dylan drilled us every day after school at his house. Sometimes Alberta and Henry helped, too, using questions from their Reach for the Top packets.

Because I'd watched the show so often, I knew the categories we should focus on: world geography, classical literature, pop culture, world history and science.

'What city was once known as Constantinople?'

'Istanbul.'

'In which U.S. state did Faulkner's *The Sound and the Fury* take place?'

'Mississippi.'

'What is the periodic table of elements symbol for mercury?'

'Hg.'

Astrid also quizzed me when I got back to the garage.

'What year did Hitler invade Poland?'

'Nineteen thirty-nine.'

'How many planets are there in the solar system?'

'Used to be nine, now it's eight.'

'Which product wanted to *teach the world to sing, in perfect harmony*?'

'Coca-Cola.'

The night before the auditions, we went to the community centre. I had a long shower. I laid out all my clothes on the passenger seat: smart trousers paired with my brand-new used red polo shirt and fresh socks. I set two alarms. No way was I going to be late.

I said goodnight to Horatio, my mom and Mel, and climbed into bed early, but I was jangly with excitement;

I got through at least ten different lists in my head before I finally fell asleep.

Then, at 6:58 a.m. – just before my alarm went off – disaster struck.

Someone was opening the garage door.

My mom cursed from her bed.

Whoever it was started banging on the side of the van and shouting in another language. I scrambled down from my bunk in my Minions pyjamas and grabbed the nearest weapon, our frying pan. Astrid, in her long johns and T-shirt, slid open the door.

The man was dressed in work clothes and work boots. He kept shouting. I didn't need to know the words to know he was angry.

'We just needed a place to park for the night,' my mom said. 'We'll go.'

The man – probably the contractor who'd been hired to finish the house – took out his phone and hit speed dial. I was so scared. Horatio looked scared, too. He ran around and around on his gerbil wheel, like he was trying to escape.

Astrid scurried into the front seat. She put the keys into the ignition. '*Tusan*,' she said in Swedish.

'What? Mom, just go!'

'We're plugged in.' She looked at me. 'Felix, we are plugged in.'

I knew what she wanted me to do. I glanced out the still-open side door. The man started talking to someone on the other end of the phone in his mother tongue. Was it the owner of the house? The police? I had no idea. He turned away from us for a moment.

I seized my chance. I leaped out of the van, ran to the electrical outlet and pulled out our extension cord. Astrid started the engine.

The man turned around and saw me. Just as I tried to scramble back into the van, he grabbed me by my pyjama top.

I bit down on his hand, hard.

He yelled. He let go. And I dived into the van.

Astrid tore out of the garage as I tried to close the side door. The man kept yelling at us, shaking his fist as we drove away.

'OK. It's OK, Lilla Gubben,' Astrid kept repeating, like a mantra. We'd driven back down to Jericho Beach and parked in one of the oceanfront parking lots. I was in the passenger seat beside her, and I was shaking.

'How can you say that? It is not OK! How do you know he wasn't calling the cops and giving them our licence plate number? How do you know they're not looking for us right now?'

'He didn't call the cops. He was probably calling the owner, or the developer.'

'But he might have copied down our licence plate, or memorised it. The owner might have told him to call the cops next—'

'Felix, stop it. Stop being such a worrywart—'

'Don't call me a worrywart! Just because I'm the only sensible one in this family, it does not make me a worrywart!'

She glanced over at me. 'Ouch.'

I started hiccuping. 'I bit him. I can't believe I – *hic!* – bit him.'

'It was self-defence.'

I caught sight of the time on the dashboard display. 'Aw, crap!'

'What?'

'I'm supposed to be – *hic!* – meeting Winnie at the – *hic!* – bus stop *right now*.'

'It's OK, Böna. It's OK.' Astrid tried to pull me into a hug.

I wriggled free. 'No, Astrid. It is not OK! None of this is – *hic!* – OK!'

She took a deep breath. 'You're right. It isn't. But for now, you need to pull yourself together. Go to the washroom and get changed. Then I'll drive you downtown.'

I started hunting for my shoes. 'Oh no. Oh *no!*'

'What?'

'My shoes are in the garage. I left them outside the van because you said they stink.' I thought of the other things we'd left behind: our lawn chairs, the space heater, our pot and our dishes.

'It's OK. You have other shoes.'

'I have – *hic!* – rubber boots.'

'So put them on.'

I slipped on my rubber boots. I got out of the van, clutching my clothes, and ran to the beachfront washrooms. The closer I got, the more I realised I really had to go. Number one *and* number two. I grabbed the door to the men's washroom and pulled.

It was locked.

I pushed, just for good measure, then tried pushing *and* pulling to make sure. Normally they were unlocked much earlier. Why, today of all days, was the unlocker of the bathroom doors late for work?

Panic rose in my throat. I was desperate.

I had no choice. I ran to a nearby tree. I pulled down my Minions bottoms.

I let loose.

There were dog walkers on the path, but they were far enough away that they couldn't see what I was doing. It didn't matter, though. I had never felt so awful.

So pathetic and worthless.

Thank God I had some old Kleenex balled up in the pocket of my hoodie. But I couldn't clean up the mess I'd left. I couldn't wash my hands afterwards. In all our weeks of living in the Westfalia, this was the first time I felt truly homeless.

Hopeless.

I pulled up my bottoms and turned to walk back to the van.

That's when I saw a woman, maybe twenty metres away from me, walking a dachshund.

One look at her face and I knew that she'd seen everything. She was gaping at me, speechless with disgust.

You think you're disgusted, I wanted to shout. *Imagine how I feel.*

Astrid drove me downtown. Traffic was bad. She tried to talk to me, tried to buoy my spirits, but I refused to answer.

I changed in the back seat as she negotiated her way through rush-hour traffic. I smeared a ton of deodorant under my arms, and a bit down my pants, which stung.

'You want me to park and come in?' Astrid asked when we finally pulled up outside the Holiday Inn with five minutes to spare. She was still in her long johns, her hair a tangled mess; she looked as close to a crazy lady as I'd ever seen her.

'No.' I opened the passenger door and climbed out.

'OK. Well. I'll just wait here for you, then—'

A wave of hot, black anger rolled over me. 'NO! Just go! I'll take the bus. I don't want to see your face!' I slammed the door shut.

And turned to find Winnie, in her canary-yellow beret, standing in front of the hotel, gaping at me.

• • •

We bounded up the staircase to the second floor. 'You're late.'

Shut up.

'I was worried. I let two buses go by.'

Shut up!

'I was texting you—'

'Look, I'm sorry. Really. It was beyond my control.'

'You're wearing rubber boots with your nice trousers. And your shirt has a little grease stain—'

'What are you, the fashion police? I *know*, OK?'

She fell silent.

For three seconds.

'I take it that was your mom,' she said as we hurried down the second-floor corridor, following the signs that read WHO, WHAT, WHERE, WHEN – AUDITIONS.

'Yes.'

'Why were you shouting at her?'

'She's the reason I was late.'

'Do you shout at her like that a lot?'

'No! Of course not.'

'Because whatever your mom did, I'm not sure she deserved that outburst—'

'Winnie, please, I beg you, just shut up.'

Her whole expression sort of imploded. She slowed her pace. Her voice quavered when she spoke. 'Did you honestly just tell me to shut up?'

I didn't answer.

'I have been raised to have a strong feminist perspective and a healthy sense of self. Therefore I cannot go out with someone who verbally abuses and bullies me.'

'Who said we were going out?'

Her eyes filled with tears.

'Winnie, come on. I'm sorry. I'm just trying to get my focus back. I've had the worst morning—'

'That's what bullies do. They make excuses. Then they do it again. Besides, the way you spoke to your own mother—'

'It's complicated! You have no idea how complicated!'

We'd reached the doors to the audition space. 'By the way,' she said, 'your deodorant is completely overpowering.'

'Who's being verbally abusive now?'

'You two cut it awfully close,' said the woman sitting at a table just inside the doors. 'One more minute and we would have turned you both away.'

'I apologise,' said Winnie.

'Me too. We're usually very prompt.' I checked out the rest of the room. It was filled with folding chairs, and the chairs were filled with kids. At least forty of them.

'I need to see some ID, and your parental consent forms.' Luckily I'd packed all the documents I'd need into a folder the night before. I handed them to her now.

The woman gave us each a badge number that we had

to pin to our shirts. 'Wait over there until your name is called.'

I sat down. There was an empty chair beside me. But Winnie took one at the other end of the room, as far away from me as she could.

My stomach started doing flips.

I got up and asked the woman at the desk if I had time to go to the washroom. She nodded, but told me to make it quick. I dashed down the hall and had a pee, then I scrubbed my hands for a good four minutes. I took a paper towel and wet it, then stuck it down my shirt and pants to wipe away some of the deodorant's perfume. I ran my hands through my hair. I tried to pull my trousers over my rubber boots so only the toes would show, but the trousers were too narrow. I knew I looked like an idiot. I told myself I'd just have to own it, pretend it was part of my look.

They called people into the audition room in groups of fours. After an hour and a half, Winnie's name was called, along with three others. I tried to give her the thumbs up on her way past, but she refused to make eye contact.

I sat waiting, trying not to think of the gnawing hunger in my gut.

About twenty minutes later, the doors opened and Winnie stepped out with two of the other kids. She wouldn't look my way. But she looked miserable.

I stood up to go to her, but the man with the clipboard came out and said, 'Alicia Jones, Sherman Wong, Felix Knutsson.'

My stomach twisted like a pretzel. I followed the other two into the adjoining room. It was bigger than the first, and they'd set up a sort of mock *Who, What, Where, When* set, with podiums for us to stand behind. There were buzzers at each spot. Two people stood behind studio-sized cameras, ready to tape us. A small group of men and women in suits sat behind a table in comfy leather swivel chairs.

Horatio Blass was not among them. I felt a surge of disappointment.

A girl from Winnie's audition, Sari, had been asked to stay behind. She stood at the podium on the far right. I was guided to one of the middle podiums. I kept my armpits firmly at my sides so as little BO and/or deodorant would be released as possible.

The man who'd led us in introduced himself. 'Hey, everyone, I'm Gouresh, head of contestant relations.' He gave us a quick lesson on how to use the buzzers.

Then one of the suits, a severe-looking woman with skin colour like mine and white hair, said, 'I'm Nazneen, one of the show's producers. We're going to do a mock round of the game. We assume, obviously, that you're familiar with the format.'

The four of us nodded. My stomach growled.

'Oops. Someone didn't have breakfast,' said Nazneen,

and the suits all laughed. My microphone had picked up the sound. I felt the blood rush to my face.

'OK, let's begin.'

The mock round lasted for what felt like half an hour, but was probably only about ten minutes.

'In what city did Romeo meet Juliet?' (Verona)

'What is the name of the river that forms the boundary between Earth and the Underworld?' (Styx)

'Which Roman emperor had a palace built for himself out of gold?' (Nero)

'What pop singer hails from Stratford, Ontario?' (Justin Bieber)

'To visit the ruins of Persepolis, you would have to travel to what country?' (Iran)

They packed in tons of questions. It took me a moment to get familiar with the buzzer, but then I was off to the races. I answered quite a few questions before the others, and almost all of them correctly. So did Sari.

The suits' expressions revealed nothing. Some of them didn't even look at us. One guy scrolled through his phone. 'OK, thanks very much,' said Nazneen. 'Sherman and Alicia, you can go. Sari and Felix, please stay.'

Sherman and Alicia slunk out of the room. Then the suits brought in two other kids from previous rounds who'd been asked to stay. We played another mock round, harder this time. This time, I was the only one asked to stay.

'We have a few personal questions for you now, Felix,'

said Nazneen. 'About your home life, your hobbies. Tell us about your family.'

'It's a small family. Just me and my mom.'

'Are you a fan of *Who, What, Where, When?*'

'Oh yes. I started watching it with my mormor when I was young. I even have a gerbil named Horatio Blass.'

The guy who'd never taken his eyes off his phone glanced up.

'No!' said Nazneen.

'It's true. I named him after the host, because it's my favourite show ever.' A couple of the suits wrote in their notebooks. Then my stomach growled loudly again. 'Sorry. No breakie. Nerves.'

'So tell me, Felix,' asked Nazneen. 'What would you do with the money if you won?'

'There's money?' As ridiculous as it sounds, I hadn't thought about money. I knew the adults played for money, but I didn't know the Junior Edition would have cash prizes, too.

'Sure. A thousand for participating. Twenty-five hundred each to the four finalists. And twenty-five grand to the winner.'

My ears started ringing. I had to grip the podium.

Twenty-five thousand dollars.

Nazneen was waiting for my answer. 'I would give it to my mom,' I said. 'To help us get a decent place to live.'

The suits glanced at each other, even phone guy. 'OK.

Thanks,' said Nazneen. 'You'll hear back from us within two weeks.' She held out a box of doughnuts that sat open on the table. 'Take one for the road.'

I grabbed a jelly-filled one, my favourite kind. 'Thank you. Thank you so much.'

I walked to the bus stop, shovelling the doughnut into my mouth. Little puffs of icing sugar cascaded down onto my trousers and into my rubber boots, but I didn't care. There was only one thought running through my brain.

Twenty-five thousand dollars.

Twenty-five thousand dollars would mean no more cold nights.

No more public washrooms.

No more shoplifting.

No more lies.

Twenty-five thousand dollars was more than enough to pay rent for at least a year.

It was enough to turn our fortunes around for ever.

It was lunch hour when I got to school. I saw Dylan at his locker and clomped towards him in my rubber boots. 'Amigo!' he said. 'How'd it go?'

'Pretty good, I think.'

'Winnie's been back for a while. With a little black cloud over her head.'

'Yeah, I don't think it went so well for her. And also, she's mad at me.'

'Why?'

'I told her to shut up.'

'Oh. Well. I can see the temptation.'

'Yeah.'

'But you should probably say you're sorry. You know, for all our sakes.'

I nodded. 'Wish me luck.'

He patted my shoulder. 'Luck.'

I walked down the crowded halls towards the cafeteria. I spotted Winnie's yellow beret in the distance. But it wasn't on her head – it was being flung like a Frisbee by Donald and Vlad.

Winnie was between them, jumping up and trying to grab it as it flew by. 'Cut it out, you guys. It's not funny!'

I felt really angry all of a sudden. Angry on Winnie's behalf, yes. But my anger felt like an octopus; it had many tentacles.

I really had grown a lot since September, because the next time Donald tossed the beret I grabbed it effortlessly in mid-air. I handed it back to Winnie.

'What'd you do that for?' said Donald. 'We were just having fun.'

I grabbed Donald's baseball cap off his head and tossed it into a nearby garbage can. 'Did that feel *fun*? Or did it feel kind of aggressive and threatening? Because maybe that's how it feels to Winnie.'

'Don't speak for me, thank you very much,' she said. Then she added, 'But he isn't wrong. It *does* feel aggressive—'

'Hey,' Donald interrupted. 'That's mine.'

'What?'

He was staring at my chest. 'That shirt.'

'No it's not. I just bought it.'

'Not new, you didn't. Look, it's got the grease stain from my bike and everything. That's why my mom gave it away. To the poor people's place.'

I felt sick. 'It's not a poor people's place. It's the Salvation Army.'

'Yeah, where poor people shop. I mean, what regular person would buy a used, stained shirt?'

Thanks to my growth spurt I had a good five centimetres on Donald. And yet I'd never felt as small as I did right then.

Winnie turned to him, her hands planted on her hips. 'You're an idiot, Donald. Tons of cool people shop at thrift shops. Not that you would know.'

Donald shrugged. 'Hey, whatever. I'm just saying, it's where my mom donates all the crap we don't want.'

'I'm surprised she hasn't tried to donate *you*,' Winnie snarled.

It was Donald's turn to look offended. He plucked his baseball cap out of the garbage bin. 'Whatever. You two freaks deserve each other.' He and Vlad walked away.

I knew my face was red. I could barely bring myself to look at Winnie. I looked at a spot on the floor instead.

'Three things,' she said. 'One, Donald's a turd. Two, that shirt looks great on you. And three, while I am partially grateful for your knight-in-shining-armour routine, it does not forgive your earlier behaviour.'

Then she placed her beret on her head and walked out the front doors.

I found her at one of the picnic tables, laying out her lunch: two sandwiches, two egg tarts, a mandarin orange, a cheese stick and a bag of rice crackers.

I sat across from her. 'Aren't you cold out here?'

She took a bite from one of her sandwiches. 'Did I say you could join me?'

'No. And I'll leave in a minute, I promise. I never should have snapped at you this morning. I'm sorry. There's just— I have a lot of stuff going on, stuff I can't talk about. But I never should have taken it out on you.'

She looked up from her sandwich. 'Why can't you talk about it?'

'I'd be breaking someone's trust.'

'Your mom's?'

I nodded. She didn't say anything, so I stood to go.

'Wait. Where's your lunch?'

'I forgot it,' I said. An Invisible Lie.

She slid one of her sandwiches and one of her egg tarts across the table. 'Eat.'

I sat back down. I was so hungry, even her bread didn't taste half bad.

'Are you?' she asked.

'Am I what?'

She kept her gaze on the table. 'Poor.'

'I don't know. Maybe.'

'That must be hard.'

'We're OK. Really. It's just temporary.' Winnie passed me half her cheese stick and half her mandarin, which I accepted without a word. 'I'm sorry things didn't go better for you this morning.'

'I tanked. I froze with the buzzer.'

'I bet a lot of smart people tanked. It was stressful.'

'How did you do?'

'Pretty good, I think.'

'What happens next?'

'They said they'd let us know in two weeks if we'll be on the show.'

She held up her bag of rice crackers and gestured for me to open my hands. Then she poured in a bunch. 'I'm happy for you,' she said.

And this time, she sounded sincere.

Astrid texted me the new location of the van. She said she was job hunting and would be home by dinner.

It was a long walk. She'd parked the Westfalia on a quiet street in Dunbar, far from the Point Grey garage. I noticed that she'd rubbed the licence plate with mud to make it less visible.

I climbed in and closed the door behind me. I took off my coat and peeled off the red polo shirt, then put on my hoodie.

I climbed back out. I walked to a nearby park and tossed the red polo shirt into a garbage bin.

'I got you these today,' Astrid said when she got back. 'I hope they fit.' She held out a pair of barely used black Converse sneakers. I took them without a word. I didn't want to know where, or how, she'd gotten them.

I continued my silent treatment throughout dinner, which was tinned stew. 'I know you're still angry with me,' she said. 'And I don't blame you. But will you tell me about your audition? I really want to know.'

'It was fine.'

'Come on, Böna. Please?' Her eyes were glistening.

I caved. I told her about the entire morning in great detail, except for the part about the prize money; I didn't want to get her hopes up.

Later, when we were lying in our beds, Astrid said into the near darkness, 'Things will get better soon, Felix. I promise.'

I used to believe her when she said that. Then for a while I thought it was more like a Give Peace a Chance.

But now? Now it felt like a Someone Might Lose an Eye.

Astrid fell into another Slump. 'I've been trying so hard to find work,' she said from under the covers a few days later. 'I don't understand why no one will hire me.'

I had my own theory: for weeks she hadn't been putting the same care into her appearance. Her clothes were wrinkled. She looked worn and haggard. Her wavy hair was unkempt. If I could see all these things, so could prospective employers. But all I said was, 'I don't understand, either.'

A Give Peace a Chance.

Then I came down with a nasty cold. The stress, dampness and lack of sleep had finally done a number on my normally excellent immune system. Even though I felt like death warmed over I dragged myself to school, because the thought of spending the day trapped in the van with my depressed mother was too much to bear. Besides, the October edition of the paper was hitting the stands, and I wanted to see it.

This time, Winnie's article appeared first in the French section. From memory, and translated into English, it went something like this:

'You Think It Won't Happen to You'
By Roving Reporter Winnie Wu

Imagine: it is cold and rainy and dark. Instead of crawling into your warm bed in your warm house, you crawl onto a piece of cardboard in a doorway, huddled in a filthy, mouldy sleeping bag, just trying to get some shut-eye and not get shooed away or beaten up. This is the life of Bob the Bard. He's been homeless for twenty years, and, as he says, 'You think it won't happen to you. But it can happen to anyone.'

And it can! Did you know that Bob the Bard used to have a regular job? He went to university. He had a wife and kids. And now look at him! A few unfortunate events and *wham!* But so many of us look at him like he is not one of us, like he is barely human, instead of someone who got down on his luck and stayed down. Our mayor and our premier talk a lot about ending homelessness, but talk is not action! Talk the talk and walk the walk, politicians!

As for the rest of us, let's try to be kinder! Because — I'm just being frank here — I have noticed that certain people in our very own school are not very nice towards those who may be less fortunate than them. But you know what? Just because you have less money does not mean you're

```
a lesser person. In fact, sometimes the
more money you have, the more of a jerk
you are! . . .
```

Et cetera. The article took up one and a half of the three French pages. My crossword and 'Fun French Facts' article (on the invention of the hot-air balloon) and Dylan's follow-up piece on poltergeists were squeezed into the remaining space. We didn't mind, because we both knew this was Winnie's dream. She beamed with delight every time someone complimented her. 'Thank you,' I heard her say at one point. 'I plan on being a world-renowned journalist, and this is one small step towards my goal.' Ah, Winnie.

But as the morning wore on, my cold got worse.

'Dude,' Dylan whispered to me at one point, 'you sound like you have emphysema. You should *not* be at school.'

I knew he was right. But where else could I go?

When the bell rang for lunch, Monsieur Thibault asked me to stay behind. 'You sound awful, Felix. I have to recommend you go home and rest.'

I nodded.

'Speaking of home. Is everything OK?' He said this in English, which made me nervous.

'Yes. Why?'

'You don't seem yourself lately.'

'Everything's fine. I'm just sick.'

He studied me for a few moments. 'OK. Go on, then. Go on home.'

What home? I wanted to scream.

I didn't go back to the van. I just couldn't deal with Astrid. Instead I went to the library and fell asleep at one of the study carrels.

I woke an hour later to a rustling beside me. I glanced up, still bleary-eyed. An old guy was sitting in the study carrel next to mine. He was staring right at me, a huge grin on his face. Then I realised where the rustling sound was coming from.

He had his thing out, and he was holding it in his hand.

I leaped up and ran out of the library. I wandered down Broadway, feeling shaken and weak. I went into Kidsbooks and flipped through books for a long time. The staff was nice and didn't make me feel like I was loitering. I felt bad that I was probably leaving my germs on the pages.

My stomach felt raw with hunger. All I'd eaten for breakfast was a mealy apple.

I walked west, past Ahmadi Grocery. Fruit and vegetables were piled high out front, including bananas. I love bananas.

I thought about my ledger, back in the van. Surely it would be OK if I took one banana – just one – and wrote it down? After all, I was going to pay them back eventually for the other items my mom had stolen.

I glanced around. The man who worked there – I assumed he was Mr Ahmadi – was unloading a box of oranges. I picked up a bunch of bananas, yanked one off and stuffed it into my coat pocket. Then I started to walk away, remembering Astrid's advice to try to look calm.

A large hand gripped my shoulder. 'Young man, you had better come with me.'

Mr Ahmadi marched me past his wife and took me into a tiny, cramped room at the back of the store. He stared down at me, arms crossed over his barrel chest. 'I'm sorry,' I said. 'I'm so sorry.' I was shaking, both from my cold and from fear. 'I won't do it again, I promise. I've never stolen anything in my life.' This was true. My mom had stolen plenty, but I had not.

'Give me your parents' number. I am going to call them.'

'Do you have to?'

'Yes, I do. It seems to be the only way to get through to you kids that stealing isn't a joke.'

I gave him my mom's phone number.

'What's your name?' he asked as he started to dial.

'Felix. Felix Knutsson.'

'There's no answer,' he said.

That's because she's in a Slump, I thought. 'I'll try her on my phone. She'll answer if she sees my name come up.'

I dialled. Mr Ahmadi gestured for me to hand him the phone. 'Hello, is this Felix Knutsson's mother? . . . I just caught your son stealing a banana . . . Ahmadi Grocery on Broadway . . . Yes, that's right . . .' When he got off the phone he said, 'She'll be here in half an hour.'

He perched on the small desk. 'Do you know how often neighbourhood kids try to take things from us? They think it doesn't matter. But my wife and I, we work hard. Seven days a week. We make a living, but barely. When people steal from us, it hurts. We are the ones who have to cover those costs, and our margins are small enough to begin with.'

I felt so ashamed. 'I'm really sorry,' I repeated.

'Why did you do it? A dare? Just for fun?'

I shook my head. 'I was hungry.'

He looked me up and down. 'You are skinny like a rake. Do you get enough to eat?'

'Yes,' I said. 'Most of the time.'

'Hard times at home?'

'Just a rough patch.' Suddenly my stomach growled. It sounded extra loud in the quiet room.

Mr Ahmadi passed me the banana. 'Eat.'

I tried to eat it slowly. But I was so hungry I wound up wolfing it down. Mr Ahmadi's expression was unreadable. 'Don't move.' He left the room. I could see him talking to his wife.

A moment later, Mr Ahmadi returned with two large plastic-wrapped muffins. 'My wife says you would be doing us a great favour if you could eat these. The sell-by date is today.'

I ate them both. They were delicious. 'Thank you.'

Astrid arrived a few minutes later. She looked like she'd just woken up. 'He stole a banana?' she said to Mr Ahmadi.

'That's right.'

'How much does a banana cost? Fifty cents?' Astrid pulled out her change purse. She took her time, putting nickels and dimes on the counter while the three of us looked on. I could tell she was trying to make a point, and I hated her for it. 'There. There's your money.'

'Astrid,' I said. 'Stop.'

'All this fuss over one lousy piece of fruit.'

Mrs Ahmadi stiffened. 'It isn't just about the fruit,' she said. 'Your boy is hungry.'

Astrid's fierce expression wavered; she had no retort for that. 'Let's go,' she said to me. She turned to leave.

Mr Ahmadi fixed his gaze on me. 'Stay strong, Felix.'

I felt like they could both see right through me. And that freaked me out, so I just hurried after my mom.

NOVEMBER

A week passed and Astrid's Slump showed no signs of letting up. It was her longest yet. 'Are you taking your pills?' I asked her one morning.

'No.'

'Why not?'

'Had to make a choice this month. Phone bill, or pills.'

I looked after her as well as I could. I made our meals and gave her pep talks. But I also stayed away from the van a lot. I became a fixture at Dylan's, to the point that one night Mrs Brinkerhoff insisted on talking to my mom. I called Astrid and handed her my phone. I could hear snippets; Astrid gave the performance of her life. 'Working long hours at a new job . . . grateful to know he's welcome at your house . . . so glad our boys have reconnected . . . I'll have you for dinner as soon as things settle down.'

Whenever I could get Wi-Fi, I checked my phone for any word from *Who, What, Where, When*. So far, nothing.

One evening I heard Astrid on her phone as I neared the van.

'Now's not a great time,' I heard her say. 'I'm swamped at this new job.'

Lie.

'I can ask him. But he's awfully busy at school.'

Lie.

'I think he's on a field trip this weekend.'

Lie.

I slid open the door to the van. Astrid looked caught.

'Who are you talking to?' I asked in a loud voice. Loud enough that whoever was on the other end would be able to hear me.

Astrid forced a smile. 'It's Daniel.'

My dad.

Daniel is – was – my mom's best friend. After Original Felix died, Astrid moved to Toronto to get as far away from the memories, and her parents, as possible. She went to U of T, her third attempt at higher education. She studied anthropology. On a whim, she took a couple of evening classes at the Ontario College of Art and Design.

That's where she met Daniel Palanquet. Daniel is two years younger than my mom. 'He could speak fluent French. He was utterly gorgeous. He was funny, kind, everything I ever wanted in a man,' Astrid told me. 'Except he was gay.'

Astrid has told me the story of their friendship many times. They hit it off right away. She dropped out of the University of Toronto and enrolled in OCAD full time. The two of them moved in together, living illegally in a warehouse space that was supposed to be for work use only. There was no shower, just a toilet down the hall that they shared with other artists, and a sink that only had a cold-water tap.

But they didn't care. They were happy. They were *artists*. They hosted huge parties. And they loved each other.

'We were like a couple in every way. Well. *Almost* every way, if you catch my drift.'

Astrid sometimes overshares.

Daniel stood by my mom through everything. She had a lot of Slumps in the first few years after Original Felix's death. He'd make sure she ate and got dressed, but he also didn't tell her to just buck up, or smile, or try to look on the bright side. He understood that it wasn't that simple.

Things went really well between them for years. They weren't having any luck getting galleries interested in their work, but they told each other it was only a matter of time till they both got their break.

Then Daniel met a man who was twenty years older than him, named Yves. He moved into Yves's house in an area of Toronto called Cabbagetown. Astrid wasn't very nice about it. She made a lot of cracks about the guy's age, and his wine collection, which was worth more than their rent for an entire year.

She was totally jealous. She says so herself.

A few months later, Daniel and Yves went to Paris for two weeks. Daniel convinced Yves to let Astrid house-sit. He thought he was doing her a favour letting her stay in a house with hot water, a well-stocked fridge and a big TV.

When they came back, everything seemed fine. But over the next few days they realised Yves's expensive cashmere scarf was missing. As was a very, very old bottle of wine, worth thousands of dollars.

They found the bottle in the recycling bin. When Daniel confronted her, Astrid admitted she'd gone into the off-limits cellar one night, plucked it out and drank it.

Daniel probably could have forgiven that. After all, she didn't know just *how* expensive the wine was. But she also told him she had no idea where Yves's scarf was. So when Daniel dropped by the warehouse unannounced one day and saw the scarf hanging on a hook by the door, he lost it.

'I don't know why I did it,' Astrid says every time she tells me the story, which she does whenever Daniel pops, briefly, back into our lives. 'We didn't talk for a long time.'

A year went by. Astrid shared the same warehouse space with a string of other people, but none of them lasted for more than a couple of months. She missed Daniel.

'I never thought I wanted a kid. But when I turned thirty-one my biological clock started ticking. None of the guys I knew were even close to father material.'

One day, Mormor called. Astrid's father, Fredrik, had died of a heart attack.

Even though she had a love/hate relationship with her mom, Astrid knew she couldn't abandon her. She made arrangements to transfer to Emily Carr University of Art and Design in Vancouver. It was time to go home.

It was also time to swallow her pride and reach out to Daniel.

They met at their favourite bar. She apologised, for real.

She told him about her dad. They sat in the bar for five hours, catching up.

She waited until their third get-together to ask him to be her sperm donor.

'I told him I could think of no better genetic material for fifty per cent of my child.' She also told him he wouldn't have to be involved; she would raise the child on her own, wanted it that way, and didn't want a penny in financial assistance. By this point Daniel and Yves had broken up, and Daniel was working as a gallery assistant, so he didn't have any money to give.

I don't know why he agreed. All I know is that he did, because I'm the living proof. I don't know the details of how, exactly, the transaction went down, nor do I want to. I just know that they signed some sort of legal papers, and a few months later, Astrid was back in British Columbia, living with Mormor and pregnant with me.

Daniel came to Vancouver shortly after I was born and brought a huge gift basket full of baby clothes. He told Astrid that I looked like E.T. Since then, I've seen him once or twice a year, when he travels out west. He still makes art; from what I've seen it's mostly sculptures that look a lot like Rubik's Cubes. But he hasn't sold many pieces, so he still works as a gallery assistant to make ends meet.

I like Daniel. I like knowing he's out there, even if he is, as Astrid says, 'a nineteen-year-old boy trapped in a forty-year-old man's body.' Sometimes, when she's being really unkind, she calls him my Sperm Donor Dad.

I don't like it when she calls him that. Me, I usually just call him Daniel. I mean, if I don't call my mom Mom, there's no way I can call him Dad.

But when I climbed into the van and Astrid handed me the phone, I said, 'Hi, Dad.' Just to get up her nose. It worked; her lips screwed into a little knot.

'Felix, my man. I just landed in Vancouver. Sorry this is so last-minute, I'm here for a job interview. But Astrid says you're going away on a field trip—'

'Nope. I'm here.'

'Great! Can we have brunch on Sunday?'

I love brunch. Brunch is the best invention ever. Breakfast and lunch combined – what's not to like? 'Absolutely.'

'I invited your mom, but she says she has plans.'

I locked eyes with Astrid when I answered. 'That's right. She can't make it. It'll be just the two of us.'

'Are you guys still living near Burnaby? I don't have a car, unfortunately.'

'It's OK. Just pick a place and I'll meet you there.'

'I'm staying in the West End. Want to go to the Elbow Room?'

'Sure.'

'Eleven?'

'Perfect.'

'All right. See you then, kiddo. I'm looking forward to it.'

'Me too.'

Astrid was gazing at me when I hung up. Her forehead was creased with worry.

I just stared right back at her without blinking until she looked away.

We lay in our beds that night, listening to the relentless rain. 'Felix,' Astrid said into the darkness. 'I know you're mad at me. And I don't blame you. But please, don't tell him anything. I'll fix this, I will.'

I didn't answer.

'If you tell him, it might set things in motion, things we can't stop.'

I watched my breath float through the air. My nose, the only part of me that was poking out from my sleeping bag, was cold. I'd wrapped a towel around Horatio's cage before it got dark, hoping to help keep him warm.

'You could be taken away from me,' she said.

'Maybe I want to be taken away from you.'

Neither of us spoke after that.

It was a cruel thing for me to say. But I didn't take it back. Not even when I heard her crying softly, her face buried in her pillow so I wouldn't hear.

But she was about three feet away from me, so good luck with that.

The Elbow Room is a truly original Vancouver experience. Their breakfasts are awesome, and their waiters are sarcastic and sometimes rude. If you don't finish the food on your plate, they make you give a donation to A Loving Spoonful, a local charity that helps people living with AIDS. Their motto is *Food and service is our name. Abuse is our game.*

I knew beyond a doubt that no one would be getting a donation from me today, because I was ravenous. Plus, I had no money. But I knew it didn't matter, because Daniel always paid.

'For two,' I said to the waiter at the door. He was tall and lean with spiky hair. He grabbed a couple of menus and led me to a table near the back.

'Coffee?'

'Tea, please. With lots of milk.' I slid into my seat. I'd made up my mind the night before that even if it meant betraying Astrid's wishes, I would tell Daniel the truth. On the bus I'd calculated roughly how much money we'd need to pay the first month's rent plus a deposit on a small apartment, plus two more months as a buffer while Astrid tried to get another job.

I was going to ask Daniel for a loan of five thousand dollars.

My stomach roiled just thinking about it.

The waiter plunked a pot of tea in front of me a few minutes later. I filled my cup halfway, then added a bunch of milk for the calories, and four packets of sugar.

Eleven came and went.

At quarter after eleven, Daniel still hadn't appeared. I took out my phone to see if he'd texted. The battery was dead. I hadn't thought to bring my charger.

'Kid, you going to order or what?' asked my waiter. His name tag read QUENTIN.

'I'm meeting my dad. He's late.'

'Well, he has five more minutes before I give this table to someone else. I've got to make a living, you know.'

I felt a rush of panic. All I had with me was my bus pass. I wondered if they'd let me wash dishes to pay for the tea, the way you sometimes saw in the movies.

At 11:20, Daniel still hadn't shown up. Quentin slapped down the bill for the tea on the table. 'OK, kid, hit the road. Pay at the till.'

I'm ashamed of what happened next.

Tears filled my eyes. They must have been lurking really close by, because they appeared immediately, plopping one after another onto the table.

Quentin's snarky tone disappeared. He slid into the seat across from me. 'Hey. What's wrong?'

'I don't have any money. My dad was supposed to pay. He was supposed to be here at eleven.' My stomach grumbled loudly.

'Look, you sit here as long as you want.' Quentin stood up. 'I'm sure he'll be here soon. In the meantime I'm bringing you the Lumberjack, OK?'

'But I can't—'

'Don't talk back to your elders,' he said sternly.

His kindness made me want to cry all over again.

I was shovelling a fourth piece of bacon into my mouth when Daniel burst through the door, bringing a gust of cold, wet air with him. It was 11:40. He shook the raindrops from his hair, which is curly like mine but black and cut much shorter. 'Felix, I'm so sorry I'm late,' he said as he made his way to the table.

I stood up and he gave me a bear hug. He was wearing black jeans and a black leather jacket. I could feel his muscles; my dad works out a lot, and, like Astrid, he's good-looking. 'I texted you that I was running behind, did you get it?'

'My phone died.'

He sat across from me. 'I had a crazy night. Honestly, I'm too old for clubbing until four in the morning.'

'Oh.'

He took off his jacket. 'But enough about me. How are you?'

'I'm OK.'

'Tell me everything. How's school?'

'School's good. I'm in French Immersion this year.'

'Mais c'est fantastique! Nous pouvons parler en français ensemble. I grew up speaking French and Creole with my parents.'

'I know.' It had been one of my big reasons to want to do the programme. Daniel's dad was from Haiti, and his mom was from Paris. French was part of my heritage, and Daniel's parents were technically my grandparents. I got the impression that Daniel didn't see them much, and no one had ever mentioned the possibility that I might meet them one day. I wasn't even sure if they knew I existed. But if I ever did meet them, I figured speaking French could be a real icebreaker.

'What else?'

My home is a van. We are now officially living below the poverty line. Astrid seems permanently depressed. 'I auditioned for *Who, What, Where, When.* They're doing a junior edition.'

'That is so awesome! What happened?'

'I thought I did pretty good. But I haven't heard from them, so I don't know.'

'I bet you'll hear from them soon. I wish I could take credit for your smarts, but that's entirely your mom.' He opened his menu. 'What about *amour*? Do you have a girl-friend? Or boyfriend?'

Like my mom, Daniel makes no assumptions. 'No. Well. There's this girl I sort of like. Winnie.'

He looked up from his menu and smiled. 'Winnie. Is she gorgeous?'

'She's pretty. She's very bossy, though. And opinionated.'

'Ha! Just like your mother.'

Ew. 'I hadn't thought of that.'

'Speaking of which.' He closed his menu and gazed at me. 'How is Astrid?'

I chose my words carefully. 'She's been better.'

'Huh. I had a feeling. What's up?'

I put down my knife and fork and took a deep breath.

'Well, the errant father finally makes an appearance.' Quentin stood over our table, hands on his hips, shaking his head at my dad. 'Your son was about to have to wash dishes, you know.'

Daniel gave him a dazzling smile. 'I am suitably chastened. Could you bring me a coffee and the Hilary Swank omelette please, fruit instead of home fries?'

'No substitutions. But I have the feeling someone else will eat the home fries.' Quentin gave me a wink and took Daniel's menu. I couldn't help noticing that Daniel's eyes followed him as he walked away.

I waited until he'd turned his gaze back to me. 'She's in one of her Slumps,' I said.

'I'm so sorry, Felix. Any particular reason?'

'Well, she's out of work again.'

'Oh God, don't I know what that's like.'

My insides deflated. 'You're not working right now?'

'Depends on what you mean by *work*. If you mean creating in my studio ten hours a day, sure. If you mean work that makes money, no. But what can I say, hope springs eternal . . . I keep thinking I'll get my first solo show any day now.'

'I thought you had a job you liked. At that art gallery.'

'Nope. The gallery folded a year ago.' He saw the look on my face. 'Oh, Felix. You don't need to worry about me.'

I'm not! I'm worried about me! I shouted, but only on the inside.

'I make ends meet, barely. I tend bar, I paint theatre sets. I dog-sit for friends. It's not a bad life. As a matter of fact, what brought me out here was a job interview at another gallery . . . so you never know. If they offer it to me, and the pay's decent, maybe we'll get to see each other on a regular basis.'

'That would be nice,' I said. And I meant it. But my plan to ask my broke dad for five grand had just gone up in smoke.

Quentin brought my dad his omelette with the home fries on a separate plate, which he set in front of me. Then he and Daniel chatted for quite a while. My P.O.O. told me I was watching some serious flirting in action.

When Quentin walked away, Daniel leaned across the table and put his hands over mine. 'My job interview is this afternoon, and my flight home is later tonight. But I can change it to tomorrow if you like. I'll come over and talk to your mom.'

I shook my head. If he couldn't help us, what was the point? 'No. It's OK. We'll be OK.'

Daniel drank some of his coffee. 'Astrid is tough. She'll land on her feet. She always does.' He glanced at his phone. 'I'm really sorry, Felix, but I've got to fly.'

'No worries.'

'I wish we could see each other more often.'

'Yeah. Me too.'

When we stepped outside, Daniel pulled out his wallet. 'I know this isn't much, but I want you to have it.' He handed me two fifty-dollar bills. 'Let's keep it between us, OK? You know how touchy Astrid gets about me being involved in any way.'

I nodded. Thanked him. We hugged. Then he walked away.

The door to the diner swung open. Quentin stepped outside. 'Glad I caught you. This jerk just sent back a perfectly good Denver sandwich because the bread was "too toasted". I gave him a piece of my mind.' He held out a paper bag. 'Sandwich is just going to go to waste. I was hoping you could help me out.'

I took the bag. 'Sure. Thanks.'

We both looked down the block, watching my dad get smaller and smaller.

And I wanted to cry all over again, because something kind of big and enormous and overwhelming hit me for the first time:

Astrid and Daniel were great people . . . but they were not great parents.

I walked all the way home. It was a long walk, but I needed to clear my head.

I felt the two fifty-dollar bills in my pocket. A hundred dollars would do absolutely nothing to help us out of our current situation. So I made a decision. I walked over the Burrard Bridge and up to West Fourth Avenue. I stopped at Purdy's Chocolatier and bought a small bag of Himalayan salt caramels, Astrid's favourite.

When I got back to the van, which was on a street near Carnarvon Park, she was sitting in the passenger seat, still in her pyjamas, reading *Middlemarch*. Her face looked drawn and pale. 'Well? How did it go?'

I shrugged. 'It was fine.'

I could feel her anxiety. It filled the van.

'I didn't tell him anything.'

Her face relaxed. I handed her the Denver sandwich, which she insisted on splitting with me. It was delicious.

When we were done, I told her we needed to go to the community centre and have proper showers. 'Why?'

'Surprise.'

Astrid loves surprises – good ones, at least – so she did as she was told. After we'd showered, we drove to the Wolf and Hound, a pub on Broadway near Alma. I ordered bangers and mash and Astrid ordered a curry. She had a pint of beer, and I had a Coke. Our waitress let me plug in my phone behind the bar so I could recharge it.

I gave Astrid the chocolates at the end of our meal, which we stealth-ate while drinking tea. After paying the bill, I still had a bit of money left over.

I picked up my freshly charged phone on the way out. I had a bunch of texts from Daniel, plus three missed calls and one voicemail, all from the same 416 area code.

Four-one-six was Toronto, I knew. But it wasn't Daniel's number.

I listened to the voicemail as Astrid drove the van back to Carnarvon Park. 'Hi, Felix, this is Nazneen Iravani from *Who, What, Where, When*. I've been trying to reach you. Please call me tomorrow at your earliest convenience.

'I have good news.'

I barely slept. I made lists of the state and provincial capitals, Roman emperors, UNESCO World Heritage Sites – none of it helped. At six a.m. I gave up. I took Horatio out of his cage and we had a snuggle. Then I farted, over and over; my stomach wasn't used to all the rich food I'd eaten the day before.

At 6:15 I heard my mom stirring below. 'Good God, Felix, it smells like a rotting corpse in here.'

'Sorry.'

She cracked a window. 'You're up early.'

'Couldn't sleep.'

'What time is it?'

'Six-fifteen.'

'You could probably call her. It's nine-fifteen in Toronto.'

It was still pitch-dark outside. We put on our headlamps and put away my bed and folded up Astrid's. 'I'd like some privacy,' I said.

'I'll go do my ablutions.' She grabbed her toiletry bag and squeezed my hand before she left for the park's public washrooms. 'Good luck.'

I punched in the number. Someone picked up after the third ring. 'Nazneen Iravani.' She sounded very business-like.

'Hi, Nazneen. This is Felix Knutsson calling you back.'

'Felix, great to hear from you. I'm happy to inform you that you've been selected as a contestant for our junior edition.'

I opened my mouth. No words came out.

'Felix? Are you there?'

'I'm here.'

'Are you pleased?'

'Very.'

'Good. We were really impressed with your knowledge, and also with you as a person. Now, I'm going to email you a lot of paperwork to fill out, and a contract; it will need to be signed by you and your parent or guardian and sent back to us ASAP, OK?'

'OK.'

'We're going to tape the inaugural run of the junior edition in Vancouver. If it's a success, we'll make it annual, and bring it to other parts of Canada.'

'OK.'

'We start two weeks from today. The shows will be live and they'll be broadcast around the nation.'

'OK.'

'A driver will pick you and your parent or guardian up on Sunday the twenty-seventh of November at noon. Just let me confirm your address.' She read the address I'd put on my original online form, the same one Astrid had put on my school application.

'Yes,' I said. 'That's right.' Astrid and I could wait outside Mr Poplowski's law offices two Sundays from now.

'There will be four contestants for each day of the week. We've randomly selected the order. Your competition day is Monday. The kids who win their day on Monday, Tuesday, Wednesday and Thursday will compete against each other on Friday for the grand prize. So, time to start cramming.' Nazneen said all of this rapid-fire – clearly she'd had to repeat it to every single contestant. 'We'll be putting you and your guardian up at the Holiday Inn downtown for the duration. And because you live in Vancouver, please make sure you tell your friends and family to come on down and watch as many shows as they can as part of the live studio audience. We want a full house. Maximum energy.'

My mind stuck on certain words. *Driver. Holiday Inn.* But they were quickly replaced with the words she said before she hung up: 'Congratulations, Felix. You could walk away with twenty-five thousand dollars.'

Astrid stood at a sink in the women's washroom, wearing her bra and washing her pits when I flung open the door. 'I'm a contestant! I'm going to be a contestant!' My excitement dimmed a little when I saw how thin she was; I was so used to seeing her in layers of sweaters these days, I hadn't noticed just how much weight she'd lost.

Astrid's face blossomed into a huge smile. She grabbed me and pulled me into a hug. 'Felix, that's wonderful, congratulations!'

'Aargh, my head is touching your bra!'

She let me go and pulled on her shirt. It was one of her job-hunting tops, which made me feel hopeful. 'I'm so proud of you,' she said.

'The grand prize is twenty-five thousand dollars! If I win, we could find a place. We could invest some of the money. You'd have time to get back on your feet, and we'd still have money left for a rainy day.'

Her smile vanished.

'And even if I don't win the whole thing, I get a thousand just for participating. If I'm a finalist, I get an additional twenty-five hundred. That's three thousand five hundred dollars! Enough for the first month's rent and a deposit. No matter how you slice it, it comes up golden.'

She looked at me in the mirror. 'Felix. That's your money. Whatever amount you get, it's yours.'

'No. It's ours.'

She just shook her head.

'Mom,' I said. Then corrected myself. 'Astrid. I want a roof over my head. I want a shower. I want a toilet. I don't want my ears to be cold all the time. I want my own bedroom. I want a door I can close.'

'I want all of those things for you, too.'

This time, I hugged her. 'You're right. It's my money, which means I get to choose what to do with it.'

'Well, hopefully it'll be a moot point. I'm back on the job-hunting trail today, so wish me luck.'

'Luck,' I said.

I walked to school with a skip in my step. Yes, I actually skipped. I'd decided not to text Dylan and Winnie with the news. I wanted to tell them in person.

I found them standing by Winnie's locker, deep in discussion. I hurried towards them. 'Guys!'

Their conversation abruptly stopped. They looked like two raccoons who'd just been caught rooting through the garbage. My P.O.O. told me something was up.

'What's wrong?' I asked.

They glanced at each other but didn't say anything.

'What?'

Winnie nudged Dylan. He began. 'I had another karate tournament on the weekend.'

'Yeah, I know, how'd you do?'

'It was in the Main and King Edward area. I was walking to the bus stop and I thought, *I'm just going to drop by Felix's house.*'

Goose bumps sprang up all over my body.

'I walked around back and knocked on the basement

door,' Dylan continued. 'You know. The basement where you said you lived.'

Oh no.

'This woman answered. She was mad. She asked why I was sneaking into their backyard.' Dylan looked me in the eye. 'I told her I was looking for Felix Knutsson.'

I looked away.

'She started going on about how she'd been so worried about you and your mom, that Astrid hadn't returned her texts, that your stuff had been sitting in their basement for months – and then she said something about your mom breaking into their house?'

Sometimes, when Horatio is scared, or threatened, he will go completely still. Like he thinks maybe no one will see him.

I realised I was doing the same thing.

'She was really worried, Felix. She wanted to know where you guys lived, but I told her I had no idea. Then she asked where I went to school, and how long I'd known you, and how did you seem. She said – she said she was worried you might not be safe.'

That snapped me out of my stillness. 'That's ridiculous.'

'Felix,' Winnie said. 'What's going on?'

I tried to gather my thoughts. 'Did you tell your parents?' I asked Dylan.

'No. I wanted to talk to you first.'

Adrenaline was pumping through my veins. Not good adrenaline, but fear adrenaline. I felt like a trapped animal. Fight or flight?

I chose flight. I walked away from them and out of the school. They shouted after me, but I didn't look back.

I walked along Broadway. I had no idea what I was doing, or where I was going. When I approached Ahmadi Grocery, I saw Mr Ahmadi outside, stacking oranges into a pyramid.

I thought about crossing the street. But then I had a different idea. I took a deep breath and I walked up to him. 'Hello, Mr Ahmadi.' My voice shook a little.

He looked down at me, his expression stern. 'Felix, correct?'

'Yes.'

'Don't you have school?'

'It's a teacher-training day.'

'Really. Isn't it strange that there aren't more kids around?'

'I was wondering if I could help you. To make up for – you know. I won't take anything, I promise.'

Mr Ahmadi looked into the store. I could see Mrs Ahmadi, reading a magazine behind the counter. 'OK.'

He let me stack oranges while he stacked apples nearby. We moved on to onions, then yams. At one point Mrs Ahmadi came out. She nodded at me, then spoke to her husband quietly before she went back inside.

'Did you have breakfast this morning?' he asked.

'Yes,' I lied. 'No.'

He held out a banana. 'It's bruised. I can't sell it. You'd be doing me a favour. I hate having to throw out perfectly good fruit.'

'Thank you.'

He shrugged. 'I know what it's like to be hungry.'

'You do?' I asked, my mouth full of banana.

'My wife and I lived in a refugee camp for two years before we came to Canada.'

'Oh. That must have been really hard.' My guilt over my small theft – and over Astrid's numerous small thefts – grew on the spot.

'Do you want to tell me the real reason why you aren't at school today?'

I looked down at my feet. 'Do you have any close friends?'

'My wife. And Oscar and Mohammed. We play chess twice a week.'

'Do you keep secrets from any of them?'

He thought about this for a moment. 'It would be easy for me to tell you no, but that would not be entirely truthful. There are certain things I don't share with my chess mates. Things from my past that I feel are best left there. But from my wife, I hide nothing.' He laughed suddenly, a big belly laugh. 'Except when I eat doughnuts at Tim Hortons. She thinks they make me fat.' He patted his stomach and laughed again. 'And they do!'

His laugh was contagious and I laughed a little bit, too.

'I don't know what your secret is,' Mr Ahmadi said. 'But

I can tell you are burdened by it. Is there someone you would like to tell?'

I nodded.

'Someone you can trust?'

I nodded.

He raised his bushy eyebrows. 'Then what are you waiting for?'

As I considered this, Mrs Ahmadi called to her husband from inside the store.

'Time for lunch,' he said, removing his gloves.

'I'll go—'

'You will not. You will eat with us. Mrs Ahmadi would be very insulted if you didn't.'

We walked behind the counter. Mrs Ahmadi had laid out a tray with sandwiches and cold drinks. 'Eat, eat,' she said. Mr and Mrs Ahmadi sat on stools; I sat on a milk crate. I ate three sandwiches. Mrs Ahmadi took away the tray and returned a moment later with a pot of tea and cookies, round and white with a pistachio pressed into the top of each one. 'Those look amazing,' I said.

'Homemade,' said Mrs Ahmadi. 'Syrian recipe.'

'Help yourself,' said Mr Ahmadi.

I had two cups of delicious sweet tea and four cookies. Then I helped Mr Ahmadi unpack more boxes of produce. When I left, Mrs Ahmadi gave me a Tupperware container filled with the cookies and a bag full of fruit. 'For all your hard work,' she said.

I left the store with the cookies and the fruit and my mind made up.

I was sick of lying to my two best friends.

It was time to try the truth.

By the time I got back to school it was almost two o'clock, so I decided not to go in. I texted Astrid. *Where r u?*

Job hunting. Home by 6.

Perfect.

I waited just outside the school's main doors. When Dylan and Winnie came out, Winnie slugged me on the arm, hard. 'Where *were* you all day? We were worried.'

'Do you have to go home right away?' I asked.

They both shook their heads.

'Good. Come with me.'

We walked toward Carnarvon Park. It was raining, but not too hard. 'Are you going to tell us what's going on?' asked Dylan.

'It's easier if I show you.' They were unusually quiet, so I tried to fill the silence. 'I've been meaning to tell you. I got a spot on *Who, What, Where, When.*'

'Felix, that's awesome,' Dylan said.

'Yeah, great,' Winnie added. But I could tell she was distracted.

It took us about ten minutes to get to the park. 'Before I show you what I'm about to show you, I need you to know that it's strictly temporary. Especially now that I'm going to be on *Who, What, Where, When.*' I pointed up ahead. 'That's where I live.'

'That house across the street?' asked Winnie.

'No. There.'

They were quiet for a moment. Dylan figured it out first. 'The van?'

I nodded. 'It's a Westfalia.'

'Wow. Um . . . Why?'

'My mom hasn't had great luck with jobs lately.'

'Oh.'

'How long have you been living there?' asked Winnie.

'Since August.'

'That's four months. That doesn't sound temporary.'

My jaw tensed. 'Well, it is. Because one way or another I'm going to win enough money to get us an apartment. I'll get at least a thousand dollars, just for participating.'

'A thousand dollars is nothing in Vancouver,' Winnie said. 'And winning – no offence, but it's a serious long shot.'

I wanted to yank her beret down over her eyes.

'Can we see inside?' asked Dylan.

'Sure.' I unlocked the side door and slid it open.

Winnie covered her nose. Astrid and I hadn't washed the sheets or our sleeping bags in a while, plus I'd farted an unusual amount that morning. 'It's just because it's been closed up all day,' I said.

Dylan didn't seem to notice the smell. We climbed inside. First I introduced them to Horatio Blass and I let them take turns holding him. Then I showed them all of the Westfalia's features. I popped up the roof to show them where I slept. 'That is so cool!' said Dylan. He looked towards the dashboard. 'No way! Mel! I totally remember your tim-tom.'

'*Tomte*,' I said.

I gave them each a granola bar and made up the table. I turned the front seats around so all three of us could sit. 'See? It's not so bad.'

Winnie cleared her throat. 'If it isn't so bad, why have you been lying to us?'

'My mom thought it would be for the best.'

'Why?'

'She's worried that if people find out, the Ministry of Children and Family Development will get involved and I'll be put into foster care.'

'Zoinks,' said Dylan.

'How come your mom doesn't have a job?' asked Winnie.

'She's had lots of jobs,' I said, feeling a prickle of irritation again. 'But they don't always work out.'

'Why not?'

'Because her bosses are jerks. And because—' I stopped. *Because she threw drinks. Because she was mouthy.* 'What's with the twenty questions?'

'I'm just trying to understand.'

'I'm not an interview subject for your next hard-hitting article, Winnie. We can't all be as lucky as you. We can't all have two parents with good jobs.'

'What about your dad?' asked Dylan.

'You have a dad?' asked Winnie.

'Of course I have a dad.'

'Where is he?'

'Toronto.'

'Does he know you're living in a van?' she asked.

'No.'

'He should. If he knew—'

'I'm fine, OK?' I was beginning to regret telling them the truth.

Winnie's brow creased. 'Felix, you're not fine. There are days when you fall asleep at your desk. There are days when you don't have any lunch and you're starving.'

'Days when you smell,' added Dylan. Coming from someone who ranked hygiene pretty far down his list of priorities, that stung.

But before I could respond, the van door slid open. 'Well, hello!' said my mom.

Astrid smiled broadly. Too broadly. I wondered how much she'd overheard. 'Dylan, it's nice to see you. My goodness. How you've grown.'

188

'Hi, Ms Knutsson. Long time no see.'

'Please, call me Astrid. And you–' she turned to Winnie – 'you must be Winnie.'

'Nice to meet you, Felix's mom.'

'I see Felix has been showing off our temporary digs. Once the fumigators are done, we'll be able to move back into our apartment. In the meantime, we're having fun, aren't we, Felix?'

The silence went on for a long time. 'Um. Astrid. They know. Dylan stopped by Soleil's house on the weekend.'

A flash of anger – or maybe fear? – flitted across Astrid's face. 'I'm sorry, how do you know Soleil?' she asked Dylan.

Dylan threw me a look. 'Um, I didn't. I don't—'

'It's a long story,' I said, giving my mom a pleading look. *Please don't make this worse in front of my friends.* 'I can tell you later.'

The tension settled on us like a heavy blanket.

Winnie cleared her throat. 'Well, nice to meet you, Mrs Knutsson—'

'*Ms,*' Astrid corrected her.

'We'd better get going. Right, Dylan?'

Dylan took Horatio out of his coat pocket and handed him to me. 'Affirmative.'

They climbed out of the van. Astrid stood by the open door, her teeth bared in what was meant to be a smile but instead looked like something out of a horror movie.

Winnie put a hand on my arm. 'See you tomorrow. We'll talk more then.' It sounded like a threat.

It probably was.

I told Astrid everything as we walked around the park. The more I told her, the faster she walked, until, when I finally reached the end, I was struggling to keep up.

'What did Dylan tell Soleil?'

'Not much. He just asked if I was home. Soleil figured it out.'

Astrid pushed her hands against her forehead. *'Fanken!'* she yelled. A dog walker looked our way, even though she'd sworn in Swedish. 'What did Soleil say?'

I hesitated. 'I don't know.'

'Felix. Don't even try to lie to me. You've proved you're no good at it.'

'Maybe I don't *want* to be good at it, Astrid! Maybe I don't actually think that's an awesome skill to have!' The rain had started to pick up. Astrid still had on her coat; I was in my ancient I HEART GERBILS T-shirt.

'Just – please tell me what Soleil said.'

'She said she'd been trying to get in touch with you. She said she was pretty sure you'd broken in. She said—' I stopped.

'She said?'

'She was worried about me.'

Astrid ran a hand through her hair. 'Oh, that's rich. That's just rich. She had a full-time nanny who practically raised those kids, and she questions *my* parenting skills?'

The wind had picked up, too. My T-shirt and jeans were soaked through. I wrapped my arms around myself, shivering. 'Mom,' I said. 'I'm freezing.'

She glanced at me, like she was really seeing me for the first time. Her face crumpled. 'Oh my God. Felix, you're drenched.' She pulled her coat off and draped it around my shoulders. 'Let's get you home.'

'Home. Good one.'

She ignored that as we started fast-walking back towards the van.

In spite of Astrid's best efforts I could not get warm. She made me strip down to my underwear and crawl into a sleeping bag, then she put her sleeping bag on top of mine.

She heated up some cans of chicken noodle soup for dinner. I was so sick of soup. I was sick of food in cans. But I ate what I could, still wrapped in the sleeping bag.

While she was washing the dishes, she said, 'Did Dylan tell Soleil what school he goes to?'

'I think so, yes.'

'So she knows what school you go to.'

'Yes.'

'I don't trust her, Felix. She could try to make our lives miserable.'

'I think you mean *more miserable.*' I couldn't help it.

Astrid either didn't hear my dig or pretended she didn't. She put the dishes away in the little cupboard. 'I think it's best if you change schools.'

'No.'

'It'll take a little bit of doing, but I can get you transferred somewhere else. Maybe we should consider another town. Maybe somewhere on Vancouver Island—'

'No. Absolutely not, no way.'

She sighed. 'It's not really your choice, Felix. I'm still the parent here.'

I snorted. 'Could've fooled me.'

She didn't answer.

'I'm *happy*, Astrid. Not with this –' I swept my arm around the van – 'but with school, with French, with my friends. You can't take that away from me.'

'I'm just trying to keep us safe.'

'Are you? Maybe you're trying to keep *you* safe. I'm not sure that you're thinking about me much at all.'

She looked stung. 'That is not true. You're all I think about.'

'Then please, please listen. I am not going anywhere. If you try to make me, I'll run away. I'll tell my friends. I'll tell my teacher.'

'And you'll be put in a foster home—'

'At least in a foster home I'd have a freaking toilet!'

She was quiet for a moment. Then the waterworks started.

I stayed where I was. I didn't want to hug her. I didn't want to touch her.

'I'm sorry, Felix. I've tried so hard. I hope you see that none of this is my fault.'

I thought about that. Then I said what I was thinking. 'Well. Maybe not *none* of it.'

That made her cry even harder, but I didn't take it back.

I woke up the next morning with a cough.

'Maybe you shouldn't go to school,' said Astrid as she handed me a mug of hot lemon tea with honey. I could tell she was feeling guilty, which suited me just fine.

'And do what, stay in the freezing-cold van all day? Yeah, that'll help.'

She sighed. 'I suppose that as a master of sarcasm myself, it should not surprise me to see you've become so good at it.' She rummaged around in one of the cupboards and pulled out a container of six grocery-store muffins. She handed me two of them.

'Did you pay for these?'

'Of course.'

'You'll understand why I'm skeptical.'

'Felix. Enough.'

When I arrived at school, Winnie and Dylan were already waiting for me by my locker. I took a deep breath and strode up to them like nothing was wrong. 'Hey,' I said.

'Hey,' said Dylan.

'Can you shove a bum so I can get into my locker?'

They moved over. Neither of them said a word.

'I know, I know,' I said. 'You're in awe because your friend got onto *Who, What, Where, When.* Suddenly I'm like a celebrity, and you're speechless in my presence.'

Dylan laughed a little. 'I *am* super stoked for you.'

'It is very good news,' Winnie admitted. 'But—'

'*But* you also want to tell me that you'll do anything you can to help me prepare for the show, which is only two weeks away.'

'Definitely,' said Dylan. 'I told Alberta and Henry last night, and they totally want to help.'

I felt a twinge in my duodenum. 'You didn't mention the other stuff, right?'

'Of course not.'

'But about that other stuff—' Winnie began.

I slammed my locker door. 'We're going to be late for class.'

Winnie pursed her lips. 'Felix, quit prevaricating. "Prevaricating" means—'

'"To beat about the bush, be evasive." I know what it means. Might be a question on the show—'

'Felix!' Her voice rose an octave. 'You are homeless!'

I glanced around, terrified that someone had overheard. 'I am *not* homeless.'

'You live in a van. A smelly, leaky van.'

'There is only one leak, and it's a small one.'

'You can't keep living like that.'

'And I told you, we *won't* keep living like that—'

'How do you know? What is your mom doing to fix things?'

'She's looking for work.'

'But you said yourself, she can't keep a job. Has she asked for help? Like, for social housing or welfare or something?'

'No, because as I keep telling you, this is temporary. And besides, my mom has a lot of pride.'

'So she's *proud* that her kid has been living in a van for close to four months? Proud that she can't hold down a job? Proud that you're not eating properly?'

My entire body was trembling, I was so mad. I looked to Dylan for support; so far he hadn't said a word.

He just shrugged. 'She has a point, compadre. Quite a few points.'

'Your parents aren't perfect, either,' I shot back.

'Far from it,' said Dylan. 'My dad tells the worst jokes. And my mom *and* my dad are terrible cooks—'

'And your house is a pigsty,' I added. Cruelly. Deliberately. Hating myself immediately.

'Dude,' Dylan murmured.

'And your dad hates your bread and just pretends to like it,' I fired at Winnie, just to hate myself even more.

Winnie's bottom lip trembled. 'That is all different, and you know it.'

'Whatever the two of you may think? Astrid is a great mom.'

'Is she?' asked Winnie. 'Is she really?'

'Winnie.' Dylan said it like a warning.

Winnie opened her mouth. Then closed it. I assumed that for once in her life she'd decided to think before she spoke. She took a deep breath. 'I still think we should talk to someone. Like Monsieur Thibault. He'd know who to get in touch with—'

'NO!' I felt the familiar ball of panic rise in my throat. 'If you tell, they could take me away. Make me change schools. I might lose my mom for ever. She needs me. I need her. I told you because I didn't want to lie to you any more, but if you tell . . . our friendship will be over. I will never speak to either of you again.'

'Remember in third grade, when I wore socks outside for recess?' said Dylan. 'And I stepped in dog poop? And we tried to flush my socks down the toilet and flooded the bathroom?'

I nodded.

'We made a pinkie promise that afternoon to never rat each other out,' he continued. 'So I won't tell.'

Both of us looked at Winnie. She hesitated. Then she said, 'OK, fine. But only until you're done with the show. After that, if things haven't changed – I make no promises.'

'I can live with that,' I said.

After all, by the time the show was over, our problems would be solved.

I started studying my butt off. I'd never been as focused and driven about anything in my whole life.

Luckily I didn't have to do it alone. Dylan and Winnie made an announcement in class about my spot on the show, and Monsieur Thibault declared that for fifteen minutes each day, my classmates would ask me skill-testing questions in French. They all got into it, except for Donald, who would ask me stuff like, 'Spell *testicle* backward,' then burst into fits of giggles.

After school I'd head to Dylan's, where he, Winnie and sometimes Alberta and Henry tested my knowledge on art, novels, scientific discoveries, history, geography, wars, chemistry, maths, pop culture, flora and fauna, constellations, current events, spelling – you name it, they'd thought of it.

'Who wrote the 1897 classic *Dracula*?'

'Bram Stoker.'

'What drug invention drastically reduced illnesses and deaths caused by bacterial infections?'

'Penicillin.'

'What was infamous Chicago gangster Al Capone finally imprisoned for?'

'Tax evasion.'

'Where was he imprisoned?'

'Alcatraz.'

'When was Archduke Ferdinand assassinated?'

'Nineteen fourteen.'

'Be more specific.'

'No idea.'

'June twenty-eighth, nineteen fourteen.'

At five o'clock we put on *Who, What, Where, When* and I tried to guess the answers before the contestants. Winnie couldn't help shouting out answers, too, and she'd smile smugly every time she beat me to it.

Dylan let me use his dad's home office to print out the contract Nazneen had emailed. It was super long and super boring. I gave up reading it after the first page. Instead I forged my mom's signature for expediency's sake, scanned the relevant pages and emailed them back to Nazneen.

I also apologised to Dylan about twenty million times. 'I love your house,' I said again one afternoon when we were nuking pizza pops in the kitchen.

'Dude—'

'I don't know what happened, I just wanted to be mean—'

'Dude, it's OK, I'm over it—'

'You're, like, the best friend I've ever had—'

Suddenly there was a muffled *boom!* Dylan opened the

199

microwave – the pizza pops had exploded. It was cheese and tomato sauce carnage. 'See?' said Dylan. 'That was Bernard's way of telling you to shut up.'

I didn't bother pointing out that he'd accidentally punched in thirty minutes instead of three to warm them.

I liked Dylan's explanation better.

Winnie and I met with Charlie Tuyen. 'I won't be able to write anything for the November edition,' I said.

'No probs,' he replied. 'We'll just have a shorter French section this month.'

'That won't be necessary,' said Winnie. 'I'm going to write a feature article. It will require a lot of space.'

'What's it about this time?' asked Charlie. 'Climate change? World hunger? Genocide?'

'All excellent suggestions, but no. I'm going to write about Felix.'

This was the first I'd heard of it. 'What *about* me?'

'About you being a contestant on the most popular game show in Canada, dodo.'

'I can't believe I'm saying this,' said Charlie, 'but that's a great idea.'

'Goody!' Winnie replied. Then she grabbed my hand and squeezed it. I squeezed back.

She still irritated me.

But she also made me feel warm and happy at the same time.

• • •

Most nights I wouldn't get back to the van till around eight o'clock. Astrid was usually already in her bed, layered up, reading by the light of her headlamp. Our conversations were brief. 'Want me to quiz you some more?'

'No, thanks. I'm quizzed out.'

'Understood.'

'How's the job hunt going?'

'Good, good.'

'Any leads?'

'You'll be the first to know.'

Her voice had that telltale flatness, and I was pretty sure she was in a Slump. But I couldn't dwell on it. Not when I had work to do.

Not when I held the answer to our problems in my hands.

Then, with just a week to go before the game show, I got sick.

Really sick.

My cough turned into a fever and diarrhoea. Having diarrhoea is no fun at the best of times. Having diarrhoea when you're living in a van, well . . . let's just say it stinks. Literally and figuratively.

On Tuesday morning I tried to get up and I almost fainted from the effort. Astrid refused to let me go to school. 'I'm taking you to a doctor.'

She drove me to a walk-in clinic. 'Definitely a nasty flu virus,' the doctor told us, keeping her mask on her face the whole time. 'Make sure he gets plenty of rest, plenty of liquids. If it gets worse, call me.'

Astrid parked the van at Spanish Banks so I'd have a view of the ocean. She put me into her bed and piled all the sleeping bags and blankets we owned on top of me. It was a cold, rainy day. She forced me to drink a ton of water and Gatorade, and placed a bucket on the floor. 'For any bathroom emergencies,' she said. 'Don't think twice, Felix, I won't mind emptying it.' She started putting on her shoes.

'Where are you going?'

'To buy us a new space heater.' She placed her hand on my feverish forehead. 'I'll be back in half an hour.' She climbed out of the van, locking the doors behind her.

I took Horatio out of his cage and put him on my chest. He sniffed my face. He'd seemed off lately, too – like he was in his own miniature Slump. He was lethargic and hadn't been eating much. I kissed his furry head and slipped him back into his cage.

I drifted in and out of sleep for the better part of the day. I had crazy dreams. Astrid and I were in a palatial mansion, wandering through the vast rooms with Horatio Blass himself. He told us it was ours. But then he turned into Horatio the gerbil, and the whole house started to sink, because it was built on a swamp. Soon we were walking through oozy muck and trying to escape but the muck was like quicksand, and then I heard a creepy laugh. It was my *tomte*. He'd come to life, and he looked gleeful as we continued to sink—

I woke with a start just as the muck reached my waist. 'Astrid?'

She wasn't back yet. I managed a glance at my phone. It was past one in the afternoon. Had she come back, and left again? I had no idea. I glanced over at Horatio's cage. He had buried himself under some of his wood shavings. 'I hope you don't have what I have,' I murmured. Then I dropped back into feverish sleep.

This time I dreamed about my dad. All three of us were living in a loft in what I think was supposed to be Toronto, though I've never been there. I just remember that I felt happy. When I woke up again, I was feeling a bit better, like the fever had broken. The light had faded; it was almost dark outside. 'Astrid?'

She still wasn't there. I looked at my phone. Four p.m.

I called her. It went straight to voicemail.

My P.O.O. told me something was very wrong.

A wave of fear rose up in my stomach.

I tried to send her a thought message. I tried really hard.

I sat up. I'd managed not to use the bucket all day and I didn't want to use it now. I still felt weak, but I pulled a sweater on over my pyjamas and made it to the washroom.

Back in the van I called her again.

Again, voicemail.

She'd left to get a space heater and she'd been gone for five hours.

A bunch of thoughts ran like ticker tape through my head, and none of them were good.

She's been hit by a car and she's in a hospital somewhere in a coma.

She's been raped and murdered and her body is lying in the woods.

She's left me. She got fed up and she's left.

She's killed herself.

I didn't know what to do, but I knew I had to do something. I thought about calling Dylan or Winnie, but they would have to tell their parents. I thought about calling the cops, but I imagined how angry Astrid would be if I did. Then I thought, *Dead people can't be angry, can they?* And that made me start to cry.

I lit our battery-powered lamp and unlatched Horatio's cage so I could get a bit of comfort from my furry friend.

With Mormor, it had taken me a while to figure things out.

With Horatio, I knew right away.

His little body was cold and rigid.

Horatio Blass was dead.

The door to the van slid open five minutes later.

'Mom!' I wailed, not caring that I'd called her that. I fell into her arms. She held me close, stroking my hair.

'Felix, I'm so sorry, I'm so sorry.' She was crying, too.

'Horatio is dead.'

'Oh, God. Oh, Böna. Poor Horatio. I'm so sorry,' she repeated.

'Where *were* you?'

'I went to the hardware store to get the space heater . . .' Her voice trailed off.

'Oh, Astrid. Did you try to steal it?'

She nodded. 'The owner caught me. I tried to reason with him. But he wouldn't hear any of it. He called the police. It took them for ever to get there, and in the meantime he had one of his employees watch over me in the back office. My phone had died. They wouldn't let me use their landline to call you . . . They treated me like I was a piece of garbage. When the police came, the owner said horrible things about me, that I was probably a junkie or a nutbar.'

'What did the police do?'

'They looked me up in their system. They saw I didn't have any priors, so they told me I was banned from the store and let me go.' She blew her nose loudly. 'I'm so sorry, Felix. For everything. I'm such a terrible mother.'

'No. No, you're not.' And in the moment, I meant it.

'I'm so sorry about Horatio. I know how much you loved him.'

'We should bury him.'

She nodded. 'As soon as it's light out. We'll find a special place.' She put a towel over his cage. Then she made me hot chocolate from a tin of powdered mix. When I managed to keep it down, she made me more.

'Could I read to you?' she asked. She had read to me every night when I was younger, even during her Slumps.

'Yes.'

She found my dog-eared copy of *Tales from Moominvalley*. 'You know this used to be mine as a girl.'

'You've only told me a million times.'

She read aloud for a long time. She has a good reading voice. For brief moments I was lulled into feeling like a little kid again, with no cares in the world.

Then I'd remember Horatio and start to cry some more.

She read to me until I finally fell asleep.

Of the one hundred or so nights we'd spent in the van, it was the worst by far.

But it wasn't *the* worst.

That night was still to come.

Astrid and I buried Horatio under a weeping willow near the duck pond the next morning. We shared some favourite memories. 'Remember the time he escaped from his cage in the basement apartment? And we found him two days later behind the furnace?'

'Remember when I snuck him to school in my backpack and a girl screamed cos she thought he was a rat?'

We laughed. We cried.

In total I missed three days of school. When I wasn't dozing, Astrid quizzed me for *Who, What, Where, When*. I texted Dylan and Winnie and let them know I was getting better and would be back soon. They wanted to visit, but I didn't think I could bear it. So I just neglected to tell them where we'd parked the van.

I felt Horatio's absence in a big way. He'd been a part of my life for a few years, and a part of our Westfalia life from the beginning. Even on the days when I'd dreaded coming home to the van, I'd always looked forward to seeing him. Now I didn't even have that. Without him, things felt even more uncertain.

I finally returned to school on Friday.

'You look like death warmed over,' Winnie said when she saw me.

'Thanks a lot.'

'Are you sure you're OK?' asked Dylan.

'Yes. No. Horatio died.'

'Oh, Felix,' said Winnie. She and Dylan wrapped me in a group hug.

'Maybe you should stay at my house till the show,' Dylan said.

'Thanks. But I can't. I can't leave my mom, not right now.'

'How's she doing?' asked Winnie.

I shrugged. 'I'm not sure.'

Later, in the cafeteria, they passed me a bunch of food from their lunch bags. I knew they'd both started packing extra stuff, just in case.

During maths I fell asleep at my desk.

When the final bell rang, Monsieur Thibault asked if I could stay behind.

After the last student was gone, he perched on my desk. 'Everything OK, Felix?' he asked in English.

'Yes, sir. Everything's fine.'

'You seem awfully tired lately. And you don't look well.'

'I caught a bad flu. And I've been working hard, getting ready for the show.'

He gazed at me. 'You're sure that's all it is?'

'I'm sure.'

He didn't say anything for a moment. 'How are your living arrangements, Felix?'

That's when I knew someone had spilled.

'I don't know what you mean.'

He just kept his gaze fixed on me. 'I'd like to have a chat with your mom.'

'Why?'

'Let her know I'd like to speak with her at her earliest convenience.'

'But I told you. Everything's fine.'

He started scribbling a note. 'I know you have the show next week. But ask her what day works for her the week after that. We can meet before or after school.' He handed me the note.

'But sir—'

'No buts, Felix. If I don't hear back by the end of next week, I'll have the school get in touch with her.'

Winnie and Dylan were waiting for me just inside the front doors. I glared at Winnie. 'You told. You said you wouldn't tell anyone, and then you went ahead and did it.'

Winnie looked at Dylan, who took a deep breath. 'Actually, Felix,' he said, 'we sort of both told.'

I gaped at him. I felt like Julius Caesar when he realised his old friend Brutus had just stabbed him. *Et tu, Brute?*

'Monsieur Thibault approached *us*,' Winnie continued. 'While you were away. He's noticed stuff. He asked us some questions. We didn't tell him much. But we didn't lie, either.'

'He's worried about you,' said Dylan.

'Well, he can stop worrying! You can all stop worrying, and you can all stop butting in!' I pushed open the front doors.

'Come on, Felix,' said Dylan. 'You know it's not fair to be mad at us.'

'No. No, I don't know. I never want to see either of you, ever again.' Even as the words came out of my mouth, I knew how ridiculous and childish they sounded. But I just kept on walking. I had to stay focused. It was Friday, the twenty-fifth of November. On Sunday, Astrid and I would be taken to a hotel. On Monday, I would appear on *Who, What, Where, When*. After that, one way or another, things would change.

Or so I thought.

How could I know that Saturday would be such a colossal disaster? How could I know we would wind up at the police station?

Even though we are not the bad guys.

Even though Abelard is a liar.

You'll understand why I am *freaking out*.

Here is my version of what happened, Constable Lee.

Saturday was beautiful and sunny, rare for November, so Astrid and I gave the van a really good clean. Then we drove to a Laundromat and washed everything: clothes, bedding and towels. It was long overdue. I felt ninety-five per cent recovered and I was ravenous, so Astrid bought us a box of day-old doughnuts. She ate one; I ate five.

I'd planned on having one last marathon day of studying at Dylan's house, but since I wasn't speaking to him or to Winnie, I let Astrid ask me questions instead.

By the time we got back to Spanish Banks, the sun was already low in the sky and the parking lots were starting to clear. We packed our bags for the week with freshly laundered clothes, the side door open to make our movements easier.

'Nice view,' said a man's voice. I assumed he was speaking to someone else. 'I said, nice view.'

I poked my head out the door. Two guys stood near the van, staring at my mom. They were clean-cut, in jeans and windbreakers. One guy was as broad as he was tall.

Astrid gave him a steely look, then turned back to her packing.

'Looks like you live in this thing, huh,' said the muscular guy.

'Just a weekend away. Visiting friends up the hill,' Astrid replied.

'I'm Barry,' said the muscular guy. 'And this is my buddy Silvio.' He extended his hand for Astrid to shake.

She didn't take it.

Barry's smile faded. I noticed that he never once looked in my direction. 'If you want to party tonight—'

'Already have plans. With those friends up the hill. Now if you'll excuse us.' Cold. No smile.

'Just trying to make conversation.' He and Silvio walked across the parking lot to a black Camaro and climbed in. Then Barry revved the engine in a ridiculous way. The Camaro roared out of the parking lot. Astrid looked at me and rolled her eyes.

We finished packing. Astrid had bought us a large pizza for dinner. It was barely warm any more but it was still delicious. We put on coats and hats and sat with the side door open, watching as the last bit of colour drained out of the sky. We identified various constellations when the stars came out.

'Big day for you tomorrow,' she said. 'The start of a grand adventure.' She took my hand. 'Whatever happens, I'm so proud of you.' She kissed the top of my head.

'Thanks.'

'And for the record, even if you won all the money in the world, it wouldn't come close to the jackpot I won on the day you were born.'

I groaned. 'Cheese alert.'

She put an arm around me and I leaned into her. 'Massively cheesy. A great big wheel of Gouda,' she said. 'But true, Böna. So true.'

By ten o'clock we were lying in our beds, but we were too excited to sleep. 'This will be my first time ever staying in a hotel,' I said.

'Actually, your second. When you were really little, Mormor took us to Harrison Hot Springs for a weekend.'

'I don't remember.'

'What are you looking forward to most?'

'Toilet. You?'

'Bubble bath,' she replied. 'I'm going to take a bubble bath every day.'

'Hot water.'

'Minibar.'

'TV.'

'Hotel sheets.'

'Electrical outlets.'

In the distance, I heard a car engine. A loud one, like a sports car.

'Free Wi-Fi.'

'Heat.'

The car got closer. I waited for it to pass.

'The little soaps and shampoos and lotions; I'm going to tuck them into my bag every day so they keep giving us new ones.'

'Thick towels.'

The car pulled into the parking lot.

Right next to our van.

Astrid flipped off her headlamp. We both went dead quiet.

Car doors opened and closed. Footsteps.

'Hey. Hey in there.' A voice that sounded a lot like Barry's. Except slurring.

We held our breath.

'Come on, sweetheart. We know you're in there. We saw a light.'

I lay rigid in my bunk.

We were both absolutely quiet.

'I don't think she's here,' said the other voice. Presumably Silvio. Also slurring.

Then I hiccuped. *Hic!*

No! Not now!

'I heard something,' said Silvio.

'Come on, let us in. We just want to say hi.' We could hear them moving around the van. 'I think I see someone,' Barry said. He was trying to peer through the windows.

Then he tried opening the doors.

They were locked, of course. He started pounding rhythmically on the side of the van.

I hiccuped again, but it didn't matter, because Astrid had had enough. 'Get away from here or I'm calling the cops!' she shouted.

The banging stopped.

I felt a rush of relief.

It didn't last.

'I *knew* you were in there! We brought a bottle of bourbon. Let's party!'

Below me I could hear Astrid rustling through her jacket pocket. 'Stay calm, Felix. I'm going to start the van,' she said quietly. 'And if I run one of those turd brains over, the world will be a better place.'

One of the men started to tap quietly on the window, which was almost creepier than the banging. 'Open up.'

Astrid scrambled into the driver's seat and I climbed down and got into the passenger seat. I was so scared, my whole body was shaking.

Astrid must have been scared, too, because she dropped the key.

'Hey, there you are! Hi, beautiful!' Barry pressed his face against the driver's side window, which made him look even scarier. He was stumbling drunk.

Astrid found the key. Her hands were shaking but she got it into the ignition. She turned it.

It wouldn't start. '*Förgrymmat också!*'

The van started to rock. Barry and Silvio had taken positions on either side and were pushing it back and forth. Astrid tried to start the van again. Still nothing.

Suddenly Mel the *tomte* tipped forward from the dashboard, right into my hands. I held him tight.

Please, please, protect us right now, Mel! I thought. *If you do nothing else for us, do this!*

My phone landed in my lap.

Now, maybe it had just fallen from the bunk above due to the rocking.

But I prefer to believe it was Mel.

He looked at me with his beady eyes and I knew exactly what to do.

I called 911.

November 27, 4:00 a.m.

'You and your partner arrived five minutes later, Constable Lee. And instead of arresting the bad guys, you arrested us. And here we are.' I swept an arm around the police station.

Constable Lee took her feet off her desk and leaned towards me. Her eyes were watery, and my P.O.O. told me either I'd made her sad, or she suffered from allergies. 'That was an incredible story, Felix. I'm really sorry for everything you and your mom have been going through.'

'Thanks. I guess.'

'I want you to know, we're still looking for those creeps. And you and your mom are not under arrest. We brought you down here partly for your own protection.'

'And partly because the van was reported stolen five days ago.'

'Running licence plates is a routine part of our job.'

'I wish Abelard had stayed in India for ever.'

'From what you've told me about him? I wish he had, too.' She flashed a smile.

'He's not to be trusted.'

'I promise I'll keep that in mind. But in the meantime, we need to figure out what to do with you.'

Fear gripped my stomach and squeezed. I let out a silent but deadly and could do nothing but give Constable Lee an apologetic look when the room started to reek. 'Please don't call the MCFD.'

'They've already been notified.'

'What? No! Haven't you heard a word I've said? They'll send me to a foster home. I don't want to go to a foster home.'

She rolled her chair closer to mine. 'Felix. I know your mom has had her own experiences with the ministry. And it's true that separating families was much more common when she was young. But nowadays the goal is to try to keep families together. And that's what happens, even in far less ideal situations than yours.'

'So . . . you won't separate us?'

'It's not my call to make. But I highly doubt it.' She clicked her pen a few times. 'That said, you can't go back to the van. Not if it doesn't belong to you.'

I was about to say that Abelard was a liar, and that the van did belong to us.

But I stopped.

Because I wasn't sure it was true.

In fact, if I really thought about it, Abelard, who'd always been a self-centred leech, was not the kind of guy to just give my mom his van.

'If we don't go back there, where do we go?'

She didn't answer. She was looking at something, or someone, behind her. I turned to follow her gaze. A guy with a bushy beard and a turban was walking towards us.

Constable Lee smiled. 'Felix, this is the social worker from the MCFD.' Then she whispered to me, 'Vijay's my favourite. I think you'll like him.'

Vijay and I spent almost an hour together in a small office off the main room. At first I didn't want to talk to him at all. But when he told me he'd already spoken to my mom, I had to ask, 'Is she mad at me?'

'Why would she be mad at you?'

'Because I called the police.'

'She's not mad. You did the right thing.'

I wanted to believe that. 'But I made bad things happen.'

'Like what?'

'Like losing the van, and getting people like you involved.'

'People like me?'

'Ministry people.'

He stroked his beard. 'Your mom told me she had a bad experience with the ministry, growing up.'

I nodded. 'She's a good mom. Not perfect. But she tries really hard. And she loves me, and I love her.' A massive lump formed in my throat. I had to squeeze out the next words. 'Please don't take me away from her.' I willed myself not to cry, but a couple of stray tears leaked out anyway.

Vijay leaned forward. 'Felix, I would consider removal only if I thought you were in harm's way, and nothing I have seen indicates that. OK?'

The floodgates opened. I bawled my eyes out.

The rest of my talk with Vijay went OK. He asked me a lot of questions, like 'What school do you go to? Who are your teachers? What subjects do you like best? What are your biggest worries and concerns?'

I was honest with him. I told him I worried a lot about what would happen to us.

'What do you feel would be the best help for you and your mom right now?'

'That's easy. A decent place to live.'

'Do you have any relatives?'

'Just Daniel, my dad.' I told him a little bit about Daniel: that he lived in Toronto, and that he was broke, too.

'Any friends who might take in you and your mom?'

I thought about that. Dylan's parents would probably let me stay there for a while; but me *and* my mom? Winnie's apartment barely held the three of them. 'Not really.'

He jotted things down in a leather notebook.

'What's going to happen to us?' I asked.

'For the immediate future, I will work with another agency to try to get you temporary accommodation some-where, either in a family shelter or a hotel.'

'A nice hotel?'

'As I say, it would be temporary,' he said, not answering my question. Which was pretty much an answer in itself.

'How long would it take to find something more permanent?'

'Sometimes it only takes a few months. Sometimes it takes closer to a year.'

'So we could spend a year in a not-nice hotel.'

'I'm just telling it to you straight.'

My heart was pounding really fast. 'Did my mom tell you we already have a *nice* hotel room for a week? Starting today?'

'She did.'

'Can we go?'

He smiled. 'You don't need to ask my permission, Felix. Of course you should go. It's an amazing opportunity. *Who, What, Where, When* is one of my favourite shows.'

'Really?'

'Sure. I can't believe you get to meet Horatio Blass in person.'

We wrapped up a few minutes later. When Vijay opened the door, I heard raised voices. Familiar voices.

My mom. And Abelard.

Abelard's cheek had two fresh red scratch marks. I was pretty sure I knew who'd made them. 'You never had the right to take it in the first place!' he said.

'It's the least you owed me after all your months of

freeloading,' Astrid snarled. 'God, why did you have to come back from India, you turd!'

'Cut it out, you two,' said Constable Lee. She was standing between them, and she looked exhausted.

Astrid caught sight of me. 'Felix!'

I hurried over to her. She was in her version of pyjamas: grey sweatpants and her old GIRLS JUST WANNA HAVE FUN . . . DAMENTAL RIGHTS T-shirt. She put a protective arm around my shoulder. Abelard glared at me, and I glared right back.

'Let's go over what we agreed on,' said Constable Lee. 'You, Abelard, are not going to press charges—'

'Not for stealing the van. But I might charge her with assault.' He touched his cheek.

'Just try it,' I said. 'If you do, I'll show the cops video evidence of you hitting her.'

That shut Abelard right up. It was true that he'd hit her a few times, but it was not true that I had video evidence. I confess I felt proud of myself; I'd just told a convincing lie, somewhere between a No One Gets Hurt and a Someone Might Lose an Eye.

'And you, Astrid,' Constable Lee continued, 'have agreed to remove your belongings from the van immediately.'

'Fine. Yes.'

'Abelard, we'll contact you when the van is ready for pickup.'

'I'll wait,' he said.

'No,' said Constable Lee, pushing her face close to his. 'You won't.'

Abelard left. Astrid and I were escorted to the underground garage, where the van was parked. We spent the next hour packing up our stuff. Constable Lee helped. 'You can store some of this at the station,' she said. 'Until you know your next steps.'

'Thanks,' I said.

I poked Astrid, who echoed a half-hearted, 'Yeah, thanks.'

Constable Lee left us to finish up. Astrid and I kept packing in silence.

'I'm sorry,' I said.

'For what?'

'If I hadn't called the police . . .'

She gripped my shoulders. 'If you hadn't called the police, who knows what those men would have done? To me . . . to *you* . . .' She tilted my chin up, but not very far; in the past four months I'd grown almost as tall as her. 'You did the right thing.' Then she pulled me into a hug. She held me for so long, I started to squirm.

'Stand guard,' Astrid said when she finally let me go.

'Why?'

'Just do it. Please.'

She grabbed our tool kit and lifted the passenger seat, where the Westfalia's battery is kept.

It took her two minutes to remove it. She smashed it on the ground a couple of times. Then she crossed the parking garage and dumped the battery into a big blue dumpster, wiping her hands on her sweatpants. 'My parting gift, Abelard. *Namaste.*'

When we were done packing, we took one last look through the van to make sure we hadn't left anything behind. I peered under the seats, and a flash of red caught my eye.

Mel. I pulled him out and brushed him off and put him in my hoodie pocket.

Astrid and I stood gazing at the Westfalia. 'This van's been good to us,' she said.

'It has.'

'Been our home for four months.'

'Yup.'

I don't know what was going through Astrid's mind. But even though I had no idea what the future held, I know what was going through mine.

Good riddance.

Astrid and I had been awake for just over twenty-four hours. We had two hours before we were supposed to be picked up outside Mr Poplowski's law office on Broadway.

We used the police station washrooms to change out of our pyjamas and freshen up as best we could. Constable Lee was going off shift, so she offered to drive us to the address on Broadway in her Kia. No questions asked.

After we climbed out, she handed Astrid her card through the window. 'Call any time. And, Felix, I'm rooting for you. I'll be sure to tune in tomorrow night.'

She drove away.

Astrid couldn't help herself; she snorted like a pig.

'Seriously?' I said.

'Sorry. Old habit.'

We stood together in the doorway. 'Felix,' she said. She looked at me, and I looked at her. And as crazy as it may sound, I swear that for the first time ever, we successfully thought-messaged each other. *I have no idea what will happen next. And I'm sorry.*

Let's not think about that now, I thought-messaged back. *Let's just enjoy the week.*

A black limousine pulled up to the curb. A driver in a blazer and cap stepped out. 'Felix and Astrid Knutsson?'

We nodded. He took our bags and put them in the trunk, then opened the back door for us like we were somebodies. We looked at each other, wide-eyed. And I swear we thought-messaged each other again, this time with just one word: *Cool.*

There were snacks in the limo. And drinks. I hadn't eaten since the Cheezies at the police station. We tore open bags of almonds, granola bars and chips. The windows were tinted, and we pretended we were movie stars, waving at our imaginary fans.

It took us less than ten minutes to get to the hotel. 'Excuse me, sir?' Astrid said. 'Do you have an extra few minutes?'

'I do.'

'Would you mind driving us around just a little bit longer?'

He looked at us in the rearview mirror and smiled. 'I get paid either way, so don't see why not.'

He drove us through Yaletown, then into Gastown, then along the waterfront, before turning back to the hotel. We ate more snacks and waved at more imaginary fans.

Even though we were both sleep-deprived beyond belief, even though the night before had been terrifying and even though we had no idea where we'd be living a week from now, it was so much fun.

The doors to the lobby opened automatically with a *whoosh*. A man strode towards us with a clipboard; it was Gouresh, from the auditions. 'Felix, good to see you again.' He shook my hand and turned to my mom. 'I'm Gouresh Sandhi, contestant coordinator for *Who, What, Where, When*. You must be Felix's sister.'

'Smooth.' But she smiled.

'We're excited to have you both here. You have the afternoon free. At five p.m. we'll meet on the second floor in conference room B to go over some rules. This will be followed by a group dinner at six.'

Gouresh helped us get checked in. Then Astrid and I rode the elevator up to our room on the fourth floor. She let me insert the key card.

I opened the door. The room smelled like new carpet and air freshener. There were two double beds, a desk and two club chairs with a small table between them. A flat-screen TV was mounted on the wall. A coffeemaker was on a small counter beside the dresser. Best of all, a large welcome basket full of fruit, chocolate and nuts stood on the dresser. A card was inside. *Welcome, Felix, and from all of us at the Holiday Inn, we wish you best of luck on* Who, What, Where, When – Junior Edition*!*

Astrid and I looked at each other. We dropped our

bags, leaped onto the beds and jumped up and down. Then we checked out every square inch of the room. Astrid made herself coffee and me instant hot chocolate. We ate a bunch of stuff from the basket. Astrid put all the extra soaps, shampoos and creams into her bag so the cleaning staff would leave more in the morning. We unpacked our things and put them in drawers and on hangers, and I placed Mel by the TV in spite of Astrid's protests. Then I ran myself a bath and soaked in it for a long time. When I was done, Astrid drained the water, refilled the tub and had her own bath.

Then we both climbed into our beds and slept for three hours straight.

We entered the conference room just before five. It was packed with the other contestants and their parents. I counted twenty kids total: sixteen of us had been guaranteed a spot to play, four per day, with one winner from each day going on to the final game on Friday. The other four kids were alternates, in case one of us got sick or had to leave for any other reason.

Astrid and I took the last two seats in the back row. Gouresh stood at the front with Nazneen. At five o'clock on the dot, Nazneen started to speak.

'Congratulations, everyone. You've all been selected to appear on the inaugural live weeklong special of *Who, What, Where, When – Junior Edition*. We're hoping to make it a yearly event, and we can already announce that next year's show will be in Halifax, Nova Scotia.' Two kids cheered loudly; I didn't need my P.O.O. to tell me they were from the Maritimes. 'I want you to know that making it this far is already a huge accomplishment, so no matter what happens over the next week, you're all winners.'

Nazneen ran us through the rules. Some of the stuff was obvious, like 'no swearing on live TV, or using any language that might be considered foul or inappropriate'. Some of the stuff wouldn't have dawned on me in a million years. For example, she warned parents and guardians that any signs of cheating during the show – any signalling or hand gestures or sounds from where they sat in the audience, or even excessive blinking – would mean the automatic dismissal of that contestant.

Gouresh asked us to stand up when he called our names. 'Monday's contestants are: Freddie Owen . . . Azar Farzan . . . Felix Knutsson . . . and Helen Mair.'

I checked out the others. Freddie looked stern. Azar had a big smile. Helen stared at her feet.

Gouresh did the same for the Tuesday, Wednesday and Thursday contestants. 'The winners from each of the first four games will play again on Friday, in the finale.'

Nazneen said, 'Tomorrow at one p.m. a van will pick up Monday's contestants and their chaperones. You'll be driven to the studio, where you'll have a short rehearsal to familiarise yourself with the buzzers and the set. Then, at five p.m., we do the live broadcast. Any questions?'

I raised my hand.

'Yes, Felix?'

'What about the people who don't win? Are we sent home?'

'We'd prefer it if you all stayed for the week; we'll need a lot of enthusiastic audience members for each show, especially Friday's.'

I breathed a sigh of relief. My mom and I were safe till Saturday, when we would be at least a thousand dollars richer.

At dinner, Astrid and I sat with Azar, Helen, Freddie and their parents. Azar was easy to talk to. Freddie and Helen, not so much. Freddie barely ate. 'Nerves,' he said.

I didn't have that problem. It was a Chinese buffet, and I went back three times for more beef with black bean sauce, General Tso's chicken, stir-fried rice and noodles. No way was I missing out on the meals.

I was completely stuffed by the time they brought out the desserts. But that didn't stop me from stacking a bunch of egg tarts and fortune cookies into my napkin. 'For later,' I told Astrid. She slipped them into her purse.

We were back in our room by seven-thirty.

By 7:45, I was fast asleep.

On Monday at one p.m. a van picked up our group. I wore my suit; the jacket hid the rip in the shirt. My black Converse were on my feet.

Gouresh came with us. He was the only one who talked on the drive; the rest of us, even the parents, were too nervous.

We were shown into a large studio in the basement of the CBC building. Seats for about two hundred audience members formed a semicircle around the stage, which was on a raised platform. Our four podiums were side by side at one end, and a single, bigger podium – Horatio Blass's – was at the other end.

Nazneen was already there, barking orders at a small crew of men and women. She led us onstage and guided us to our podiums. I was at one in the middle. Helen was shorter than Azar, Freddie and me, so they found her an apple box to stand on. 'The questions will appear here.' Nazneen pointed at two separate screens angled in such a way that they could be seen by the contestants and by the audience. The categories – *Who, What, Where* and *When* – were in bold letters running vertically along the side. Running parallel were five blank squares per category. 'As you know from watching the show, you don't get to pick the categories – the question order will be randomly selected by a computer, with each correct answer worth two points in the first and second rounds, three in the third. For each incorrect answer, the same amount gets deducted.'

Pretending to be Horatio Blass, Nazneen led us through a quick rehearsal, asking us ten sample questions that appeared on the board. We couldn't buzz in until the question had been asked. I knew the answers to at least six, but mastering the real buzzer was harder than I'd imagined; I was always a fraction of a second behind, and only managed to ring in twice. I could feel sweat stains expanding in my pit region, and it was still hours before the actual show.

After the rehearsal, Gouresh led us backstage to the green room, which wasn't even green. It was a dingy space with a couple of old couches and some folding tables and chairs. Bagels, cream cheese, muffins and cookies were laid out on one of the tables, along with water and juice. 'Don't forget to eat,' Gouresh advised us. 'The last thing you want is to have low blood sugar when you step out onstage.'

After my marathon binge session the day before, I'd barely eaten breakfast beyond two of the egg tarts we'd smuggled back to our room. So I forced myself to eat a bagel. Chewing was an effort. I washed it down with two boxes of apple juice and hoped it would stay down.

I thought about Dylan and Winnie. I wondered if they would come, after the way I'd spoken to them.

Freddie, Azar, Helen and I barely said a word to each other. We weren't being rude. We were simply terrified.

One hour before the show, the four of us were herded into hair and make-up. 'Just a bit to hide the zits and take away the sheen,' said the guy, Gary, as he worked on my face. A woman named Aisha blasted my curls with hairspray, sending me into a coughing fit.

Nazneen poked her head in. 'Someone's here to say hi.'

Horatio Blass stepped into the room.

I swear my heart stopped. He looked a lot like he did on TV, but kind of different, too. This might sound weird, but he looked less real in real life than he did on TV. His make-up was layered on thick, and he was much shorter than I expected. His head was enormous, and I'm pretty sure his thick black hair was a toupee. His teeth, which were white on TV, were practically blinding in person. He looked sort of like the Madame Tussauds wax museum version of himself. 'Well, hello, contestants!' he boomed. The voice relaxed me; the voice was exactly the same.

We all got to shake hands with him. He wished us luck. 'Try to relax and have fun.' Then he was gone.

Ten minutes later, back in the green room, our parents were asked to go to their seats. Astrid hugged me, careful not to mess with my hair or make-up. 'Break a leg out there, Böna. And remember, whatever happens – you are amazing for making it this far.'

Then she was gone. The next ten minutes lasted for an eternity. The only sound came from Freddie, who'd started tunelessly humming to himself.

Finally Gouresh came to get us. 'It's showtime, folks.'

Who (our very own Felix Knutsson)
What (*Who, What, Where, When — Junior Edition*)
Where (CBC building, Vancouver)
When (last night on live TV!!!)
By Roving Reporter Winnie Wu

Oh, what a night. What a fascinating, grip-
ping, heart-pounding night!

This reporter had a front-row seat for
the first round ever of *Who, What, Where,
When — Junior Edition,* held right here in
Vancouver, where Blenheim School's very own
Felix Knutsson was a contestant on live
TV. This reporter had hoped to get you an
exclusive preshow interview with Felix,
even though, for ridiculous reasons that I
won't get into here, Mr Knutsson was not
talking to her. But the show's producers
wouldn't let her anywhere near backstage
before the show, stating that 'school newspaper credentials don't cut it'. This
reporter tried to sneak back anyway but
was thwarted by a large security guard.

So the first time this reporter glimpsed
Felix was when the cameras started rolling

and his name was called and he stepped onstage. If you were watching from home you'd have seen him in close-up and maybe you would've been able to tell whether he was nervous, but from my seat he looked calm. His hair looked like a halo of blond cotton candy. The other contestants were Freddie Owen from London, Ontario; Azar Farzan, who'd flown in all the way from Saint John, New Brunswick; and Helen Mair from Gatineau, Quebec. There was a lot of applause, but there was extra for Felix, the hometown boy. Blenheim had a big cheering section courtesy of our teacher, Monsieur Thibault.

Horatio Blass was introduced and he came onstage. It was a thrill to see him in real life.

Round one of the questions began. This reporter tried to write everything down, but they wouldn't allow laptops and therefore this reporter had to scribble everything in a notebook and, well, *you* try writing that fast. So I didn't catch every last question, but here are some highlights:

What is the name of the second-highest mountain in the world? (K2)

Who wrote Twenty Thousand Leagues Under the Sea? (Jules Verne)

When was Twenty Thousand Leagues Under the Sea *first published?* (1870)

Where is Timbuktu? (The West African country of Mali)

Our Felix got off to a rough start. He seemed to be having trouble with his buzzer. At the end of the first round (with one question left on the board), the scores were: Freddie Owen, fourteen. Azar Farzan, ten. Felix Knutsson, eight. Helen Mair, six.

I know this reporter speaks for all of Felix's supporters when I say the mood was bleak during the first commercial break. We watched in silence as the hair and make-up people came running out and did a few touch-ups, mostly on Horatio. Then the studio director was counting down: 'In three . . . two . . . one.' And the show was beaming live again, to households all across Canada.

Before they got into round two, Horatio asked the contestants about themselves. Freddie shared that everyone called him 'Pud' because his favourite food in the world was rice pudding. Azar talked about once boarding a plane for Saint John's, Newfoundland, instead of Saint John, New Brunswick. Helen talked about her passion for adult colouring books.

'Felix,' said Horatio Blass when it was his turn, 'I understand you named a pet after me.'

'Yes, sir. My gerbil, Horatio Blass.'

Horatio looked straight into the camera

and raised his eyebrows. The studio audience laughed. 'Might I ask why?'

'Well, your show is my favourite. And my gerbil had a black patch of fur on his head and it reminded me of your hair.'

More laughter. 'I've never been told I resemble a gerbil before. I believe we have a photo of him.' A photo flashed on a large screen behind the contestants. In this reporter's opinion, the resemblance to the real Horatio Blass was uncanny. 'He's adorable. I hope he's watching from home.'

'Oh, that would be impossible. He's dead.'

Horatio cleared his throat. 'Ahem. On that sad note, I guess it's time for us to move on to round two!'

Now, this reporter doesn't want to take too much credit, but all the practice rounds she did with Felix — along with Dylan and Alberta Brinkerhoff, Astrid Knutsson and Henry Larsen — started to pay off, big time.

He missed the first two questions in round two. Then it was like a match had been lit underneath him. He was on fire.

Where would you find Pashupatinath Temple? (Kathmandu, Nepal)

Who discovered insulin? (Banting and Best)

When did the Russian Revolution take place? (1917)

What does the Latin phrase 'caveat emptor' mean? (Buyer beware)

Felix answered all of the above correctly.

The scores at the end of the second round: Freddie, twenty-six. Felix, twenty-four. Azar, eighteen. Helen, twelve.

It was dead quiet in the studio during the next commercial break. The contestants and the audience were on tenterhooks (if you don't know what that word means, I suggest you look it up).

It was time for the final round. Only ten questions, harder this time, and worth three points each.

What does the symbol K stand for in the periodic table? (Potassium)

Who composed The Rite of Spring? (Stravinsky)

Where in the world can you swim between tectonic plates? (Iceland)

When did the Titanic *sink?* (April 14—15, 1912)

Out of the first nine questions, Azar got one right. Helen got two. Freddie and Felix got three. The scores: Helen, eighteen. Azar, twenty-one. Freddie, thirty-five. Felix, thirty-three.

Then came the last question.

Whose assassination led to the outbreak of World War I?

This reporter's heart leaped; we'd quizzed Felix on this very subject.

Felix buzzed in.

'Archduke Franz Ferdinand of Austria.'

The score on the front of his podium jumped to thirty-six.

Our very own Felix Knutsson had won the first day of *Who, What, Where, When — Junior Edition*.

The audience — including this reporter — went wild.

Now he will be in the finals on Friday. This reporter has convinced the editor of our paper to publish a special edition to cover this incredible event.

So stay tuned!

(For the French edition of this article, please go to page 6. This reporter convinced the editor that a story of this scope and importance should be published in both English and French).

After my win was announced, I heard a sound in my ears like the ocean. Azar shook my hand and said something I couldn't hear. Freddie and Helen did the same. Horatio Blass shook hands with each of us, and my ears must have started working again, because I heard him say, 'Congratulations, Felix. See you on Friday.' His breath smelled like cigarettes. And maybe alcohol.

I could hear the audience clapping, and some of my classmates cheering. I could hear my mom whistling through her fingers.

The lights came up. A photographer took pictures.

We were allowed to leave the stage and mingle with the audience. Monsieur Thibault gave me a bear hug. 'We're all so proud of you, Felix.' A bunch of my classmates hugged me and slapped me on the back – even Donald. For a moment I worried that Monsieur Thibault would seek out Astrid, but they were on opposite sides of the room and he had to get twenty kids home on the bus. Dylan was there with his family, and Alberta had brought Henry.

'Way to go, Felix,' said Henry.

Alberta ruffled my hair. 'You did it, Bionicle Dork!' Then she laughed. 'Ha-ha-ha-ha-ha-ha-HEEE-HAW!'

Mr and Mrs Brinkerhoff hugged me, too, then they went to talk to my mom. Dylan and I had a moment alone. 'I'm so proud of you, amigo,' he said.

I gave him a big hug. 'You're a better friend than I deserve. I'm really sorry, Dylan, for everything—'

He cut me off. 'It's forgotten. I mean it. You don't have to worry about me.' He held up his left hand and discreetly pointed with his right. 'Not sure I can say the same about her.'

I turned. Winnie sat in a chair in the front row, head bowed, scribbling furiously in a notebook. She looked amazing in her red beret and blue, red and yellow plaid skirt.

I took a deep breath and walked over to her, ready to get an earful. She wore a press badge on a lanyard around her neck that read BLENHEIM BUGLE, STAFF REPORTER. I could tell it was homemade. 'Winnie,' I began. 'I want to apologise—'

She stood up and threw her arms around me. 'I'm so thrilled that you won! For your sake, obviously, but also for mine. Your win makes for a much better article.'

Oh, Winnie. My Winnie.

Nazneen and Gouresh herded us to the green room to gather our things. I felt so much lighter, because of the win, but also because things were OK with my friends.

Back at the hotel I checked my phone. I had a bunch of texts, including one from Daniel.

Way to go, kid!! It was so cool, seeing you on TV! Tell your mom you got your brains from your dad, ha-ha-ha! SO PROUD OF YOU!

At dinner Freddie was subdued, but Azar and Helen were in great spirits. 'I can't believe I'm a thousand dollars richer,' said Azar.

'And have you seen our take-home prizes?' added Helen. 'We all got a year's supply of pancake batter, microwave popcorn, spaghetti sauce, maple syrup and laundry detergent! Plus a Dairy Queen gift card, a bunch of other gift certificates, a manicure-pedicure set, some board games, and something called Turtle Wax.'

I felt so happy. So calm. I ate enough food for a small army.

When we got back to our room, Astrid turned on the evening news. There was a clip about the show, featuring me. It was so weird, seeing myself on TV. 'Is that really what I sound like?' I asked Astrid.

'Yup,' she said. Then she hugged me for the twenty billionth time and told me how proud she was of me for the twenty billionth time.

At ten o'clock we turned out the lights, but I couldn't get to sleep.

I'd just scored a thousand bucks for participating, and twenty-five hundred for the win. In less than an hour we were thirty-five hundred dollars richer.

Thirty-five hundred dollars would help us out a lot.

But *twenty-five thousand* – that would be a life changer.

And after today, I had a one in four chance.

I'd tried not to think about it too much.

But now . . .

Now I wanted it more than I'd ever wanted anything in my entire life.

The rest of the week went by at a snail's pace.

I went to all the tapings. I watched the contestants carefully. I tried to figure out their strengths and weaknesses. I got Astrid to quiz me in my spare time.

Nazneen encouraged us to invite as many people as we could to the finale, so I got in touch with everyone I knew. I tried to enjoy the free meals, but it got harder and harder to eat, and even to taste.

On Wednesday, Astrid had a private meeting with Vijay. I was watching daytime TV when she returned. 'I got my prescription filled,' she said, holding a small paper bag.

'That's good. Did you tell him we don't need to be put up in a shelter or a not-nice hotel now? Did you tell him I've already won enough money for a month's rent and a deposit?'

'It's not quite that simple, Felix. A landlord will still want some sort of proof that I can be reliable when it comes to paying the rent.' She smiled, a little too brightly. 'But don't fret; he's got a place lined up for us.'

I muted the TV. 'Where?'

'A room in a motel.'

I knew from all my studying that a motel was a *motor hotel*, meaning you could drive right up to your door if you had a car. 'What's it called?'

'The Cedar Motel.'

'That doesn't sound too bad. I mean, it has *cedar* in the name. Maybe it's close to a forest or a park.'

'Maybe,' she said, avoiding my gaze. 'I'm going to run a bath.'

My P.O.O. told me she knew more than she was letting on. Once she was in the bathroom, I punched the name into our ancient laptop.

The Cedar Motel wasn't close to nature. It wasn't even close to Vancouver. It was on a busy six-lane road. It looked super rundown. The sign outside read CED R M T L. FR E CABL TV. I Google Mapped it; it would take me at least an hour and a half to get to school by bus.

The next morning I filled a bowl with porridge at the breakfast buffet. I added three pats of butter. I brought it up to our room and put it in front of Mel.

My head told me I was being silly, but my heart told me that at this point, anything that could help me win was worth a shot.

On Thursday night I was brought onstage with the three other winners; Dragan Lukic, Flora Ocampo and Talia Shoemaker. They were all really good. Talia had a particular knack for anything historical, and Dragan was a science and technology genius. The knot of nerves in my stomach ballooned till I thought it would burst.

I barely slept that night. I stood the chance, in twenty-two minutes of live TV, to fix everything for my mom and me. We wouldn't have to worry about where we would sleep. We wouldn't have to go to a sketchy-looking motel, or wait for a year for assisted housing that, for all I knew, might be even worse. We wouldn't have to live far away from my school. We'd have enough money to eat while Astrid found a decent job.

On Friday morning I forced down some breakfast. But at lunch I couldn't eat at all.

Daniel texted at four p.m., when we were in the green room.

Break a leg tonight, Felix! Got a group of friends coming over to watch the finale!

Time slowed. At one point I swear I saw the clock on the wall move backwards. I felt light-headed, exhausted.

Finally, Gouresh walked in and said, 'It's that time. And remember: each of you is already a winner.'

That, I thought, *is a Give Peace a Chance.*

Even though I have a mind like a steel trap for trivia and facts, I don't remember much about the actual game. It sounds so weird; I was *in* the game. I was *part of* the game.

But it was like I was looking down on the entire thing, like an angel version of myself.

I remember being backstage and peeking out from behind the curtain into the audience. Every seat was taken. Monsieur Thibault was there again, along with many of my classmates. Winnie and Dylan were there with their families. And a lot of other people I'd invited had come: Mr and Mrs Ahmadi and Vijay were there. It took me a moment to recognise Constable Lee because she wasn't wearing her uniform; she was in a dress with tights and everything, and she sat next to a woman who, I found out later, was her wife, Matsuko.

I remember being called onstage.

I remember that Talia and I both took an early lead, and that Dragan started gaining on us in the second round.

I remember the last two questions:

Who was born in the village of Mvezo in South Africa on July 18, 1918? (Nelson Mandela)

When did Italy become unified as one nation? (1861)

The rest is pretty much a blank.

Except the part where I won.

Confetti fell from the rafters, all over the stage and into the audience. I stood rooted to the spot, stunned. The other contestants shook my hand. Horatio Blass did the same. 'Woo-*hooo*!' he shouted. He put an arm around my shoulder and guided me to centre stage.

'How does it feel to be the first ever *Who, What, Where, When – Junior Edition* champion, Felix?'

I was hyperventilating. I couldn't form words.

'Take your time.'

'It's wonderful. You have no idea.'

He chuckled. 'Do tell.'

'It means we're going to be OK.'

'Who is *we*?'

'My mom and I. This changes everything for us.'

He smiled. 'How does it change everything?'

The words tumbled out. 'We've been having a hard time lately. We've been living in a van. And my mom's ex-boyfriend said we stole it, but he's a liar, and we thought we were going to have to live in a motel without all the vowels –' I remembered to breathe – 'but now I have money to get us a place to live and everything is going to be all right. It's like the happiest ending ever!'

I noticed that Horatio Blass was squeezing my shoulder, hard. As if to say, *Enough*.

'Heh-heh, but, son, you do understand, you don't get the money until you're eighteen. It's held in trust until then.'

I blinked into the bright stage lights.

It took a few moments for his words to sink in.

Horatio chuckled again. 'Guess someone didn't read the fine print.'

I thought back to the contract. The contract that I'd barely glanced at before signing and sending back.

I didn't answer. I couldn't answer.

'But hey, how old are you? You've only got to wait, what, five years, and the money will be yours, with interest!'

Five years.

Five *years*.

That's when I burst into tears.

In front of a studio audience.

On live TV.

I heard someone yell, 'Cut!' The studio lights came up. Horatio's on-screen smile vanished. I thought I heard him mumble, 'I'm too old for this crap,' as he walked backstage, but I can't be sure.

I saw my mom in the audience. She looked ashen. Monsieur Thibault, my classmates, the Ahmadis, the Brinkerhoffs, the Wus, Vijay, Constable Lee and her wife – all of them gazed at me with a mixture of shock and pity.

The best day of my life had flipped, in mere seconds, to the worst. Like I'd gone through a portal to another dimension, where everything looked the same, but wasn't.

I bolted.

I dashed backstage and down the long corridor, past the green room, up two flights of stairs and out a set of doors that said Emergency Exit Only. Well, this was an emergency.

I walked back to the hotel. It was already pitch-dark at six p.m.

Fractured thoughts ran through my head.

Eighteen.

Five years.

One more night at the Holiday Inn.

One. Then . . .

Ced r Mot l.

Ced r Mot l.

Ced r Mot l.

I let myself into our room with my key. My eyes landed on Mel.

I grabbed him from his place beside the TV. I opened the balcony doors and stepped outside.

I looked over the railing to the busy one-way street, four storeys below.

It was a long drop.

I stepped back into the room to get a running start.

I took a deep breath.

I sped towards the balcony.

I flung back my arm —

And chucked Mel into the air, watching as he plummeted to the ground below.

We left for the Cedar Motel early the next morning. Vijay picked us up. I made my mom walk down the stairs with me at the Holiday Inn and out through the parking garage. I couldn't bear the thought of running into people I knew. I couldn't bear their questions, or their inevitable looks of pity. Vijay told us later that a couple of news crews had been waiting for us in the lobby, too. Maybe they were hoping I would burst into tears again.

We drove.

And drove.

I tried to keep an open mind as we pulled into the parking lot and walked with our bags towards the sign that said OFF C . At the Holiday Inn, guests were greeted with a smile. Here, the guy sat behind Plexiglas and eyed us suspiciously. He spoke only to Vijay. Big signs on the wall read DRUG USE OF ANY KIND WILL NOT BE TOLERATED and VIOLENT BEHAVIOUR WILL RESULT IN IMMEDIATE EVICTION and NO LOITERING.

A number of residents sat outside or hung out in the parking lot as we made our way to our room. A few of them stared, especially at my mom. I didn't feel afraid of them – not very, anyway – but they looked like life had been hard on them. They looked like they'd reached the end of the road.

I didn't want the Cedar Motel to be the end of our road.

Vijay opened the door to our room. It smelled of past tenants' cooking and had tons of cigarette burns on the carpet even though a sign over the TV read NON-SMOKING ESTABLISHMENT. There were two beds, a TV, a bar fridge and a hotplate for cooking.

Astrid tried to cheer me up. 'At least we have real beds here. And heating, and a toilet, and a shower.'

I couldn't answer. Yes, it had all those things. But it also had a strong whiff of sadness, like I could feel the pain of the past tenants who'd called this room home.

'I'll check in with you both on Monday,' Vijay said on his way out the door.

I couldn't even summon up the energy to say goodbye.

I spent the weekend in the room, watching TV. I ignored a bunch of calls from Daniel. I ignored Winnie and Dylan's persistent texts. Astrid was glum, too, but she could see I was in my own Slump, so she did her best to cheer me up. She went out and bought groceries with some of the emergency funds Vijay had given her. She read aloud to me, but I didn't really listen.

She spent a long time on the phone with Daniel, pacing back and forth outside our unit. I could only hear the rise and fall of her voice.

On Sunday night, there was a knock at our door. I grabbed the Gideon Bible from the bedside drawer. The locks on the door were fragile, and the door was made of plywood. I'd seen the looks a few of the tenants had given Astrid, and I wasn't taking any chances.

But it wasn't any of the other tenants.

It was Vijay.

And he wasn't alone.

Who (our very own Felix Knutsson)
What (the aftermath of *Who, What, Where,*
When — *Junior Edition)*
Where (various locations)
When (one week ago)
By Roving Reporter Winnie Wu

You've probably come to notice a certain style in this journalist's reportage over the course of our first semester together. Words like *hard-hitting* and *exposé* possibly come to mind. I've tackled asbestos and homelessness, but when I tackled homelessness, I had no idea that one of our own was among their ranks.

So today I am happy to write what some might dismissively call a 'feel-good' story. I write it with the permission of our game-show champion, Felix Knutsson. (Full disclosure: This reporter is good friends with — even the sort-of girlfriend of — the subject. But this reporter did not let him have any kind of influence over the article as that would go against her journalistic code of ethics.)

First, a recap. We all know what happened

at the end of the final game. Practically everyone in Canada found out that Felix and his mom were homeless. (Felix doesn't like me to use that word; he prefers 'between places', but this reporter has to call it like she sees it.) And we also found out that he wouldn't get the prize money till he was eighteen, which, when you think about it, makes sense, and frankly this reporter feels strongly that Felix should have done his due diligence and read the contract; that oversight is on him.

But still, I felt crushed on his behalf, and so did Dylan Brinkerhoff, who has given me permission to use his name because (a) he is Felix's best friend, and (b) he wanted to see his name in print.

And it turns out that a lot of other people in the audience felt bad, too. So guess what? Dylan and this reporter made sure all those people met each other after the show. And they talked, and they decided to have a meeting the very next day. But here is the ridiculous part: even though we were responsible for bringing all of those people together, we were not allowed to attend the meeting, because it was 'for grown-ups only'. When this reporter pushed for access in the name of freedom of the press, her very own parents rudely refused. Like they somehow thought this reporter wasn't mature enough to handle what was going on, which, as anyone who knows this reporter would agree, is utterly absurd.

But here is what came out of those meetings:

Felix and his mom were offered an apartment. It is above a store on Broadway called Ahmadi Grocery. If you and your family don't shop there already, well, what are you waiting for? They have great produce, and they are great people. They own the store and the small apartment upstairs. Their son has been living in the apartment, but he got a job in Prince George and moves out in January. Felix and his mom will move in then, and while no one would give this reporter an exact dollar figure, I am told the rent is reasonable.

I would write a much longer piece, but the editor gave me only a limited amount of space, even though I repeatedly pointed out that this story is journalism *gold.* I suppose it is a good life lesson to be reminded that one will encounter certain bosses who suffer from a lack of vision and imagination. Fortunately, I doubt the editors at *Le Monde,* the *Guardian* or the *Washington Post* have this affliction, and they are my top three picks for work once I am through university.

On that note, and only twenty words away

from my maximum word count, I wish you all a very happy holiday.

(For the French edition of this article, please go to page 6. This reporter convinced our editor yet again that a story of this scope and importance should be published in English and in French — obviously.)

'Millions of people all over the world have never seen God, but they still believe in him,' Dylan is saying. 'And I have no problem with that.' His braces are full of bits of Oreo cookies from his milkshake.

'Well, thank goodness for that, since God exists,' says Winnie. She's eating a banana split, because she thinks the banana makes it somewhat healthy. I've chosen a Peanut Buster Parfait.

Dylan puts down his spoon, exasperated. 'So why do you find it so hard to believe in the paranormal? When tons of people have actually *seen* ghosts? When there is tons of actual *evidence*?'

Winnie touches a napkin to her perfect red lips. 'The only people who've laid eyes on ghosts are kooks or crackpots looking for attention. You've said yourself, you've never *seen* Bernard.'

'Felix, my buddy, my pal, help me out here,' Dylan implores me.

We're sitting at our usual booth in the Dairy Queen. Alvin and the Chipmunks are singing Christmas carols in the background. We've stopped in for after-school treats almost every day for two weeks straight, slowly using up my gift card. *Who, What, Where, When* may not release my money till I'm eighteen, but they've given me all my other prizes, most of which are stored in Dylan's basement: boxes of microwave popcorn, spaghetti sauce, maple syrup, laundry detergent, pancake batter and Turtle Wax.

I gave Dylan's parents half of the laundry detergent and spaghetti sauce as a small way of saying thanks for letting me live with them until January. Some of the rest of it went to Soleil and her family, because they're letting my mom stay in their basement till then. When I found out Mrs Ahmadi loves maple syrup, I gave her all but one bottle. Some of the prizes make perfect Christmas gifts. I've set aside the manicure-pedicure set for Astrid. I wrapped three big boxes of microwave popcorn and brought them to Constable Lee at the police station. I ordered an enormous ice-cream cake for my class with some of my Dairy Queen gift card. And at my last meeting with Vijay, he told me about his old Mustang convertible, which he's restoring on weekends.

He got the Turtle Wax.

I even sent Daniel a Christmas gift: a one-hundred-dollar WestJet gift card, to put towards a flight to Vancouver. He sent me a gift, too: a fifty-dollar bank transfer which I know was a big deal for him. He never did get the job he'd interviewed for out here. He wishes he could help out more, money-wise. But we talk on the phone much more often now, *and* he talks to Astrid, and that counts for a lot.

Dylan and Winnie got Christmas presents, too. We did our own gift exchange yesterday, at Dylan's house. Dylan got the board games I'd won, and Winnie got a one-hundred-dollar gift certificate to Staples, so she can buy printing paper or whatever else she wants for her writing.

The two of them had to leave the room to get my gift. 'Close your eyes,' Winnie demanded before they stepped back in.

I did as I was told. 'OK,' said Dylan. 'You can open them.'

In front of me was a cage with the sweetest little gerbil I'd ever seen. Caramel-coloured, with white patches.

I got a little dewy in the eye region.

'You can call it Horatio Blass the Second,' said Winnie.

'No,' I said. 'Definitely not.'

'It's your gerbil, my friend,' said Dylan. 'You can call it whatever you want.'

I thought about it for a moment. 'I will call you Dillie,' I said to the gerbil.

A combination of the names of my two best friends in the world.

When Vijay showed up at the Cedar Motel almost two weeks ago, he was with Soleil, the Ahmadis and Mr and

Mrs Brinkerhoff. The Ahmadis told us about the apartment. For a moment I was scared that my mom's weird pride would get in the way and that she would say no to their offer. But she didn't.

The Brinkerhoffs told us I was welcome to stay in Dylan's room until January, and Soleil offered her basement to Astrid. We packed up our stuff and drove over to see the apartment. As we stood in the tiny living room, I couldn't read my mom's expression. She turned to Mrs Ahmadi. 'Why are you doing this? What's in it for you?'

My heart constricted. I think she was genuinely perplexed, but she sounded kind of hostile.

'A steady rent cheque, that's what,' said Mrs Ahmadi. Her face was unsmiling.

Suddenly Astrid grabbed Mrs Ahmadi's hand and squeezed it, hard.

Still unsmiling, Mrs Ahmadi put her other hand on top of Astrid's.

She squeezed back.

The apartment is tiny. It smells like rotting vegetables. But there are no signs on the walls telling us what we can and can't do. There are no people eyeing us with suspicion. There are no cigarette burns, and no scary sounds coming through the walls. It is clean. It has a toilet and a shower, and heating, and even a pint-sized bedroom, which Astrid has said will be mine; she will sleep on the pull-out couch.

Bob the Bard sleeps in doorways. Mr and Mrs Ahmadi spent two years in a refugee camp. *Two years.*

I tell myself I am one of the lucky ones.

Since the finale of *Who, What, Where, When*, Astrid and I have been getting a lot of mail from across the country and beyond. We got one letter that came all the way from Cockermouth, England. Dylan and I laughed over that name for a long, long time.

A few letters and tweets are nasty. They say things like Astrid shouldn't have had a kid if she can't raise him properly, or that she's just another welfare mom. But most people are kind. They write about their own struggles and wish us luck. Some of them have even sent cheques for twenty, fifty or a hundred dollars. I told Astrid I didn't feel right about keeping the money. But when we did the maths, we realised we could give the Ahmadis three months' rent up front if we cashed the cheques. So that's what we've done. We are writing thank-you cards to each and every person. And we've also allowed ourselves to buy one new set of clothes and one new winter coat each, because we need to look good for our new jobs.

A few days after the finale, Astrid got a call out of the blue from an administrator she used to know at Emily Carr. He told her that enrollment was up, and asked if Astrid would consider coming back to teach a painting class to first-year students. I have no idea if he saw the show and knew about our situation; he never mentioned it. Astrid said yes. She starts after the holidays. It doesn't pay a lot and it's only part-time, but she'll get to use their studios to paint, which is a major bonus.

My new job has already begun. It's also part-time. I work for Mr and Mrs Ahmadi two days a week after school and one day on the weekend. I only let them pay me for the weekday shifts; the weekend day goes towards the rent. A few days ago I got my first paycheque. I put half of it in the bank and took half of it out in cash. I walked to Bob the Bard's corner and bought two poems from him. Then I walked to the No Frills so I could start paying them back for the things my mom had shoplifted. But when I tried to explain, the cashier looked at me like I was crazy and told me to get lost.

I was wandering around the store, trying to figure out what to do, when I spotted an elderly woman in shabby clothes, looking through the dented, on-special cans. All she had in her cart was a box of birdseed and a tin of kidney beans. I walked up to her and held out a twenty-dollar bill. 'Excuse me. You dropped this.'

'Oh, heavens, I don't think so.'

'You did. I saw it fall out of your purse just now.'

She gazed at me with her milky eyes; then she wrapped her hand around the twenty. 'Thank you, young man. Thank you very much.'

I will keep doing things like this until I have settled up what we owe, one way or another.

• • •

Astrid and I see each other a couple of times a week. She and Soleil are trying to mend their friendship. I don't think it's going too well. Astrid complains every time we get together. 'She judges me without saying a word.'

I tell her that's the pot calling the kettle black, and that she should put up or shut up.

Sometimes I get these waves of anger towards her, and it makes me feel bad. But I see Vijay once a week, and he lets me talk about all my emotions. It helps.

To be honest, it hasn't been the worst thing, getting a break from my mom. But I only tell that to Vijay. When Astrid asks if I miss her, I always say yes.

A Give Peace a Chance.

Dylan and Winnie are still arguing loudly in the DQ. 'How do you account for all the stuff Bernard has done? Felix has seen some of it, too.'

'Earth to Dylan,' says Winnie. 'Has it honestly never occurred to you that "Bernard" is actually—'

'Anyone want a bite of my Peanut Buster Parfait?' I interrupt. I grab Winnie's hand across the table and shoot her a warning look, which she thankfully understands.

'I'm just saying,' Dylan continues, 'there's no difference between you believing in God, or me believing in Bernard, or Felix believing in his tim-tom.'

'*Tomte*,' I correct. I reach into my coat pocket and put

my hand on Mel. After I threw him off the balcony I felt immediate regret; my mormor had made him especially for me. So I ran down four flights of stairs, found him lying on the pavement, and carried him back to the room.

I have another mouthful of Peanut Buster Parfait. A beam of sunlight hits our table. Right here, in this moment, I am filled with happiness, sitting with my best friends, eating ice cream, listening to them argue.

I get why Winnie believes in God. I get why Dylan believes in Bernard. I get why I wanted to believe in Mel. It can give a person comfort, feeling that something mysterious and otherworldly is looking out for you.

But now I'm learning to have faith in something new. Something my mom stopped having faith in a long time ago.

Other people.

Astrid didn't have much luck with them, growing up.

But I am not my mom.

And I am choosing to believe.

Acknowledgements

I have oodles of people to thank for helping me bring this story to life. Quite a few of them have helped me many times, still picking up the phone when they see my name on call display. Randy Fincham, the Vancouver Police Department's media liaison, is prompt and insightful. Catherine MacMillan, who was my son's guidance counsellor through high school and now guides others with her compassion, wit and smarts – ditto. My husband, Göran Fernlund, reads my manuscripts, sometimes multiple times, without complaint (perhaps he realises it makes for a happier marriage). Same goes for Susan Juby – she is one of my favorite authors, and I can't believe I not only get the gift of her excellent feedback, I also get to call her a friend.

Thank you to Alex Scheiber, Deputy Director of Child Welfare at the Ministry of Children and Family Development in British Columbia, for taking the time to answer my questions. And to Social Worker/Counsellor

Amanda Oliver, your insights were invaluable. While I sit in front of my laptop and make stuff up, people like you are out there trying to make the world a better place for those who find themselves vulnerable.

I had a great deal of fun interviewing people who've either created or been on game shows. John Brunton, CEO at Insight Productions, has produced a lot of game shows, and he helped me tremendously. I was tickled to find out that my talented author/radio personality friend Kevin Sylvester was once a contestant on *Canada's Smartest Person* – his stories were hilarious and helpful. And thanks to another author/radio personality, J.J. Lee, for putting me in touch with Julie Backer, who was a real, live contestant on my favourite game show, *Jeopardy!* Julie and I had a great discussion over dinner; I loved hearing her insider tales! I also enjoyed reading *Prisoner of Trebekistan* by Bob Harris. I must also give a shout-out to Janette McIntosh, who kindly toured me through her VW van and showed me all the bells and whistles.

I had quite a few "advance readers" for this manuscript, each of them offering unique and invaluable perspectives. Léonicka Valcius, Rania Barazi, Liz Johnson-Lee, and Ellen Wu (no relation to Winnie – at least, not that we know of): I owe you each a heap of gratitude. You helped me get to know some of my characters even better. Katie Wagner seemed to know an inordinate amount about living in a van. . . . She gifted me the bit about having to "unplug" before tearing away from the garage. ☺ And a special shout-out to my young readers: Martin Cassini, Isabella Harrison, Noah Poursartip, and Forrest Rozitis. Your comments were deeply appreciated, and I was grateful that you saw the humanity in Astrid; as one of you said, she is a "let-down mom".

To my wonderful agent, Hilary McMahon – can this really be book six?? Thank you for your skills in guiding and building my new career. Working with you for the past ten years has been nothing short of awesome.

I feel thoroughly blessed to have three exceptional editors/publishers, who gave me such in-depth, thoughtful feedback on this manuscript at every draft. Tara Walker, my lead editor – well, anyone who's worked with Tara knows it's hard to put into words, even for a writer, what her notes and before-and-after conversations mean to the quality of the end product. She always pushes me, in the kindest ways, to dig deeper, and to explore nooks and crannies that I would never have thought of on my own, but always in a way that stays true to my vision (sometimes, though, my vision is blurred, and I need help bringing it into focus). To have the added gift of Wendy Lamb in the US and Charlie Sheppard in the UK – well, it's like the icing *and* the whipped cream on top of the cake; these extraordinary women know how to drag better stuff out of me every single time, and I am for ever grateful.

Dana Carey, Peter Phillips, Chloe Sackur, Colleen

Fellingham: thank you for your keen eyes and VAT (value-added tips). There are so many others I would like to thank at Tundra, Penguin Random House Canada, Wendy Lamb Books, Penguin Random House US, and Andersen Press – I still pinch myself that I get to work with this incredible group of people, who have such a passion for books.

Lastly, it took me a while to find the proper ending for this story. Sometimes ideas strike at really odd times. In this case, it happened when I was at West Point Cycles in Vancouver. My husband and I love road biking. While he was in the store looking for something, I wandered, lost in thought. . . . Suddenly the ending burst into my brain, and tears sprang to my eyes. The owner of the shop, Tim Woodburn, asked if I was OK. I told him I was better than OK, I'd just figured out the theme of my book, and the ending. He said since it happened in his store, I should mention them in my acknowledgments. So here it is: Thank you, Tim and Sara Woodburn of West Point Cycles – you guys are awesome in so many ways.

The Inspiration for
No Fixed Address

Unlike most of my books, I know the exact moment that I first had the idea for this one. I was lying in a hotel room in Kelowna, BC, where I was doing a series of school visits in February 2015. It was four a.m., and a lingering cough had woken me up. I was drifting back to sleep when the thought came, 'I should write about a boy who lives in a van with his mom.' I had the wherewithal to write the line down when I got up a couple hours later, then set it aside, as I was deep into another manuscript.

I suspect that initial idea had sprung from a couple of things:

1) Anyone who lives in Vancouver – or in any other large, internationally renowned city – can't help but be aware of the growing housing crisis. Homes and land are increasingly treated as commodities and investments. Housing prices have skyrocketed. Rental units in Vancouver are scarce and costly, and renters are constantly being evicted as older

homes are torn down at a rapid rate, replaced by large homes that – to add insult to injury – often stand empty. More and more citizens are being pushed out of the city, or pushed to the brink of poverty and despair. The lack of political action at every level is disheartening.

2) I briefly met a couple many years ago who told me that while he was in university, they and their school-aged daughter had lived out of a van. They talked about it like it was a great adventure. But a small (judgemental) part of me thought, 'Was it *really* a great adventure for your kid? Like, in the dead of winter? When she's older, will she talk about it to *her* kids like it was a great adventure, or will she talk about it to her therapist? Or both?'

There were elements of this story that I only realised I'd been hungry to delve into once I'd begun writing. First is that gradual awakening kids have, that their parents are far from perfect. I loved writing Felix, who defends his mom until he can't any longer. Second, I wanted to write a deeply flawed parent. I, too, grew up with a single-parent mom. I, too, was an only child. But unlike Astrid, my mom was a stable, steadying force. We were far from wealthy, but we never worried about eviction, or about where our next meal would come from. Astrid is a strong woman who loves her son deeply, and many of the misfortunes that befall them are not directly her fault. But she has been damaged by her past, and doesn't always make the best choices. As one of my young readers said, 'She's a let-down mom.' Third, I don't know why, but I've always wanted to have a game show in one of my books! This was my chance.

Lastly, while this book is entirely a work of fiction, I did lift one story from a certain someone who shall remain nameless . . . Felix's humiliating moment, when the bathrooms at the beach haven't been opened yet . . . let's just say that happened to someone I know while that person was out on their morning run . . . Enough said about that. ☺

Thank you for taking the time to read.

Sincerely,

Susin Nielsen

No Fixed Address
Discussion Questions

- *No Fixed Address* opens with Felix agreeing to tell his story up until now to Constable Lee, on the November night before he is due to go to the hotel. The story then goes back in time to the previous summer. How does this affect your expectations as you read the book? Can you think of other examples of stories (whether novels, films or television) where this device is used?

- Felix tells the story of Astrid's childhood and her life up till now. What events from her past do you think have contributed to her situation in the novel? What could she have done differently, if at all?

- The novel is told from Felix's point of view. Discuss the reasons why the author, Susin Nielsen, chose to tell the story in this way.

- Discuss Dylan and Winnie, Felix's two very different friends. In what ways are they similar and different?

- Felix makes lists in his mind as a coping mechanism for his difficult and lonely life. Look at the different kinds of lists that appear in the book, for example in the chapters 'A Brief History of Homes' and 'Astrid's Guidebook to Lies'.

- We aren't told until halfway through the full story of Felix's dad, Daniel. Why do you think Felix takes so long to tell the reader about him?

- Felix finds Winnie deeply annoying when he first meets her at school, and tries to avoid including her to begin with. Discuss how his feelings towards her change throughout the book.

- *No Fixed Address* has many characters who turn out to be very different to what Felix or the reader thinks at first. Compare one main character and one minor character and the ways in which they defy expectations when we learn more about them.

- Discuss the themes of shame and guilt in *No Fixed Address*.

- *No Fixed Address* takes a look at the lives of the 'hidden homeless' – the people who are without a permanent home and are just about finding alternatives to sleeping rough on the streets. What aspect of Felix's precarious existence would you find hardest to deal with?

The Hidden Homeless

No Fixed Address is a story about the 'hidden homeless' – people who do not have a permanent home, but don't sleep rough. They may instead find places to stay with friends or family, sleeping in spare rooms, basements or on sofas; or they might be on a waiting list for social housing for a long while, living in hostels or bed and breakfasts that the local authority provides. Not having a permanent home to call one's own makes normal life very difficult: it can make it harder to find a job or a school, or to make commitments; there are often financial and social burdens; and not having a proper bed can affect health and mental wellbeing. Many people who live such precarious lives feel embarrassed and want to hide the fact that they are in difficulty.

If you have been affected by the issues in this story, or if you would like to find out more about how you can support people without homes, the following organisations may be able to provide help and advice:

UK:		Ireland:	
Shelter	www.shelter.org.uk	Focus Ireland	www.focusireland.ie
Crisis	www.crisis.org.uk	Threshold	www.threshold.ie
Childline	www.childline.org.uk	ISPCC Childline	www.childline.ie
	Helpline: 0800 1111		Helpline: 1800 66 66 66

Amnesty International UK endorses *No Fixed Address* because it upholds our right to a home and a reasonable standard of living. We all need homes, shelter, food, clean water and access to health services and education. These are human rights and they are the foundations of a decent life. Yet hundreds of millions of people worldwide live in extreme poverty and there are many homeless and undernourished children even in rich countries. Governments have a legal duty to prioritise the most disadvantaged people, but they do not fulfil this.

Amnesty International is a global movement of millions of ordinary people standing up for humanity and human rights. We try to protect people wherever human rights values like equality, justice, fairness, freedom and truth are denied.

Human rights are universal and belong to all us from birth because all countries of the world have signed legally binding human rights treaties. Human rights help us to live decent lives that are fair and truthful, free from abuse, fear and want and respectful of other people's rights. But they are often abused. We need to be alert and to stand up for them, for ourselves and for other people. We can all help to make the world a better place.

You can take action for people at risk at www.amnesty.org.uk/actions

Find out how to start an Amnesty youth group in your school or community at www.amnesty.org.uk/youth

If you are a teacher or librarian, you are welcome to use our free human rights education resources at www.amnesty.org.uk/education

Amnesty International UK, The Human Rights Action Centre,
17-15 New Inn Yard, London EC2A 3EA
Tel: 020 7033 1500
Email: sct@amnesty.org.uk
www.amnesty.org.uk